Alternate Endings

Short Stories of Speculative Fiction

Lesann Berry

Isinglass Press
SILVERLAKE, WASHINGTON

Copyright © 2013 by Lesann Berry.

All rights reserved. No part of this publication may be reproduced, distributed or transmitted in any form or by any means, including photocopying, recording, or other electronic or mechanical methods, without the prior written permission of the publisher, except in the case of brief quotations embodied in critical reviews and certain other noncommercial uses permitted by copyright law. For permission requests, write to the publisher, addressed "Attention: Permissions Coordinator," at the address below.

Isinglass Press
P.O. Box 1731
Castle Rock, Washington 98611

Publisher's Note: This is a work of fiction. Names, characters, places, and incidents are a product of the author's imagination. Locales and public names are sometimes used for atmospheric purposes. Any resemblance to actual people, living or dead, or to businesses, companies, events, institutions, or locales is completely coincidental.

Cover Design by www.Humblenations.com
Interior Design by www.BookDesignTemplates.com

Ordering Information:
Quantity sales. Special discounts are available on quantity purchases by corporations, associations, and others. For details, contact the "Special Sales Department" at the address above.

Alternate Endings / Lesann Berry. -- 1st ed.
ISBN 978-1-939316-02-8

For Those Who Take the Road Less Traveled

No success or failure is final.

–ANONYMOUS

Table of Contents

1   Like Sunlight on Seawater

9   Messy Business

17   Call of the Muezzin

25   Adventure in the Caldera

43   Find Yourself in Maui

49   Blind Mary

63   The Beast Within

73   If You Build It…

81   Late for Life

91   Crossing the Water

105   The Unexpected End

111   Like Shadow in Moonlight

1 Like Sunlight on Seawater

AFTER MONTHS OF visiting sales rooms in the art district and scouring the antique shops along the historic center of town, Cassie found what she'd been seeking at the legendary bohemian flea market in Soho. The right accent piece came in the form of an exquisite transparent blue vase. She pushed her way through the crowd, holding her breath as she slipped past a cluster of bare-chested young men who stank of sweat and beer.

The aqua colored glass caught her eye from across the aisle, but on closer inspection, the opaque milk white interior added an unexpected depth of tone. Certain she could not afford the beautiful thing, she asked anyway. The vase offered the exact finishing touch to the entry of her apartment. Approaching two feet in height, the shape would create a dramatic visual statement against the sheen of ecru walls and mahogany plank floor. Atop the antique rosewood letter desk, the vivid color was sure to lure the eye of every visitor, not that she had any yet. She'd lived in New York since May and already dreaded working the night shift during the long winter. As an EMT with junior status, treating accident victims on her knees in freezing slush was something she didn't anticipate with relish, but the perks on living in the city were too amazing to pass up. She'd inherited the tiny apartment from an aged aunt; otherwise she'd never be able to afford the posh address.

The aged vendor smiled at her excited interest but instead of quoting a price, he asked her a question. "Do you believe in fate?"

Cassie didn't pause to think, she nodded. "Sure. There's got to be some divine order to the universe, right?"

He stared at her for a long moment and then said, "fifty bucks."

She asked him if he knew where the beautiful piece came from a she hurried to extract three twenties from her wallet, anxious to hand over the money before he changed his mind. Her fears were unfounded.

His features became even more animated. "My wife brought this with her from Greece. She claimed the vase had been in her family for generations." He wrapped the glass in layers of newspaper. He paused at his task, glancing up to catch her gaze. "When you grow old like me and find yourself alone after many years of marriage, material things don't mean so much. I'll use this money to visit Florida during the cold months." With careful movements he tucked her purchase inside a white paper sack. Grizzled brows rose as he held out the parcel. "My wife claimed an ancestor carried this precious thing from Constantinople, across the waters, to Crete." He hesitated a moment. "She meant to pass it along to our daughter but the Lord blessed us only with sons."

Cassie grasped the raffia-wrapped wire handles. On impulse, she reached out and squeezed his veined hand, felt the fine trembling in his fingers. "I'll treasure this like she would have wanted."

His lips curved into a little smile. "Then I know my wife's treasure goes to a good home. May it bring you a wealth of blessings."

A gust of heated wind soughed through the aisle of vendors, whipping ebony curls in front of Cassie's eyes. She brushed back her hair, caught the flush of satisfaction in the old man's features and felt pleased.

With an almost imperceptible squeeze of his fingers, he pulled out of her clasp, turning to answer the inquiry of another customer.

Thrilled with her treasure, Cassie departed. She walked with the sack suspended from her right hand, enjoying the late summer sunshine. The air felt oppressive as she trudged along the wide sidewalk. Soon the weight dragged at her wrist. She transferred her grip from the handles to the bag itself, hugging the bulk against her chest and supporting the fragile object from underneath. Six blocks later the parcel felt so heavy she flagged down a taxi, climbed inside and settled the package on the seat beside her, tucking it secure against her thigh. She'd gotten such a bargain on the vase she'd splurge on the cab ride.

At home she washed and dried the vase in the kitchen sink; half believing it might be an antiquity. A delicate tracing of etched whirls curled along the edge of the rim where years of accumulated grime had obscured the tiny patterns. In the foyer, she set the vessel on the smooth polished wood, stepping back to admire the effect. Under the incandescent bulb, the glass glowed as though lit from within. The color reminded her of sunlight on seawater, and she caught herself wondering if the blue matched the hue of the Aegean Sea.

"Everything I ever wanted." Cassie whispered, running a fingertip down the glossy surface of the jar.

The next morning she readied for her daily run, anxious to stretch stiff muscles and exercise away the lingering images of disjointed but erotic dreams. Bouncing on the balls of her feet, she limbered up her calf muscles, prepared to shave a minute off her the first mile. It wasn't until she'd entered the hall and saw her aunt's antique rosewood table that her normal routine collapsed.

Instead of the pristine condition she'd left the vase in last night; the urn was a seething mess. Viscous fluid oozed over the smooth lip of the jar and trickled in a thick line along the side of the blue-green glass to puddle around the base. Dark as ink, she recognized the ichor for blood. As she watched, a wave of droplets slithered down to join the spreading stain. Under her horrified stare the fluid coalesced, became stronger, heavier and weightier. A glint of something white rolled over and nudged a turgid lump. She thought the material might be bone. A tumescent mass of tissue wavered at the vase rim before falling, splatting into the wetness with a soft plop.

Cassie swallowed.

Her stomach churned.

Panic climbed her throat.

Arms crossing her torso, and fingers digging into the taut flesh covering her ribs, she leaned low to peer at the morass as a spherical ovoid rose from the pool. Black threads began to sprout above the protuberance. A bulge of red-streaked whiteness broke the surface and spread outward in a smooth arc. The round shape halved. The upper lifted to reveal an orb.

It was a human eye.

A whistling moan seeped from Cassie's paralyzed throat but the sound carried mere yards.

The optic, rich and deep as Turkish coffee swiveled. The eye rotated until it focused on her and blinked.

Cassie inched back, the soft soles of her running shoes making no noise on the bare wood flooring.

The process of creation accelerated. A maelstrom of cruor and gore spun. Osseous matter poked from the distillation. Mass extruded from the top of the vase as though pouring from some ancient fount of life.

Shuddering in deep breaths, Cassie retreated back down the hall and by the time she reached the halfway mark, a man sprawled on the dainty rosewood structure. He cradled the fragile vase against his chest. There was not a trace of blood in sight; all had been absorbed into his spare frame.

She rejected the panic bubbling in her mind. What was the sense in panicking? She knew she'd just witnessed something impossible. Faced with the reality that a naked male stood between her and the front door, Cassie retreated a step. By the look of things, in another minute the man from the vase would find his bearings and stride the distance separating them, maybe even ask for a drink of water.

Or strangle her.

Or throw her on the floor and...do something.

From down the length of the hall Cassie could see his fixated attention never strayed from her. Eyes of burnt umber, deep-set below slashes of brow, balanced his saturnine features. His skin, the color of late-harvest honey, smoothed over the ripples of his ribcage where the line of his hip curved into his flank. His body was rigid and well-defined, reminiscent of a conditioned athlete.

All good, she concluded, except for the little fact that this excellent specimen of maleness had spun from nothingness and spilled out of a jar like some monstrous creature of myth.

A college memory clicked. She recalled a class schedule loaded with comparative literature, world religion and mythology. A nugget of information concerning Djinns surfaced. If her recollections hadn't confused history with fantasy, they were a type of supernatural entity that attached themselves to objects inherited through bloodlines.

Like the preternatural vase carried across the Aegean Sea.

Check. And check.

One tiny promise to treasure a dead woman's artifact and bam, it was like she'd hydrated a package of sea-monkeys and got a bonus human male.

A hot one.

ALTERNATE ENDINGS

The man stepped to his feet, positioned the vase on the pristine wood and splayed one long-fingered hand on the wall. His eyes never left her. He staggered forward, muscles sliding flawlessly, each step steadier. Gorgeous, exotic and naked, his smile suggested a need.

Cassie didn't think he was thirsty.

Pulse accelerated, winded as if she'd run her two-mile route twice, she stood transfixed as he approached.

He loomed over her. Sinewy arms snaked around her waist. The heated press of his physique brought a rush of sensation and a palpable sense of synchronized connection inside her.

A soft moan escaped Cassie but her thoughts were blank, her body sang with tension, aching like a singular taut nerve-ending.

Warm palms slid along her sides, down her ribs to embrace the curve of her hips, his fingers curling around with a firm grasp. Bending low, the man's lips feathered a trail of kisses up from the pulse of her throat until he paused to whisper in her ear. The words were little more than a warm exhalation of air but they resonated deep within Cassie.

"Wish granted."

2 Messy Business

E VERYONE ELSE REMEMBERS it as the day the saucers came, but in my mind that will always be the night a man in a spacesuit shot my father. Funny how events can change the direction of your life isn't it?

The first saucer appeared in the sky over New York, minutes after midnight. The date was a Tuesday, the tenth of August. Since we live in the Pacific Standard time zone it took us a bit to figure out the clock difference. In our defense, being stoned complicated things. The invasion happened while Dave and I were busy doing our usual, pounding shots of Jagermeister and smoking a baggie of Jamaican Blue. We'd scored the weed off some dude in West Hollywood and missed the first round of panic. We got back to Dave's house just as one of those special news reports interrupted the rerun of our favorite flick. The party atmosphere kinda flopped after that.

We hunched on the couch and watched as the television displayed similar images from around the globe. People say that every major metropolitan area feels the same and the sole difference I could see was the shape of the skyline. The squared-off steeples of skyscrapers jabbed skyward like so many punctuation marks, pointing at the disks hovering above every major metropolitan area. The news announcer jabbed at a map illustrating winking dots of light that represented the spaceships sprinkling the length and width of the country. The red lights created a crazy hodgepodge of connect-the-dots.

Dave speculated whether or not the design formed a giant arrow from space and made me laugh, the sound emerging a little maniacal. The laughter bubbled up my throat and left a rancid layer of saliva slicked across my tongue.

"C'mon Jeremiah, dude, check out this shit!" Dave charged out the front door.

I followed him outside and found the sky filled with familiar shapes. I wasn't surprised. Sooner or later this had to happen. I mean, everyone should have been expecting aliens to show up at some point. Carl Sagan had been pointing out the probability for like five decades. Dad always said invasion was inevitable. I just didn't think it would be today. Wrong again.

Another message vibrated against my ass. Dad was just two blocks away, but he kept texting my phone and demanding I come home. Urgency scratched inside my chest but my eyes fixated on the soft blue and green lights rotating around the circumference of the craft overhead. To the naked eye, the UFOs were much more beautiful than they'd appeared on television. The web of interlacing beams flowed like the acid tracers I'd experienced at the Metalheads concert we'd crashed in June.

I stumbled off the bottom step, bumping into Dave. We stared up, watching as the disk sank lower and lower until a single ship blanketed the entire Los Angeles basin. The impossible scale of the shiny exterior glowed white as neon, a perfect sphere back-dropped against dark blue. I thought the saucer looked like a silver dinner plate of spinning perfection, reminiscent of bad "B" movie posters, the kind lining the windows of the tourist shops on Hollywood Boulevard.

Then I was running toward home, my sneakers retracing the path I'd followed thousands of times over the years. I darted between the trashcans lined up in a neat row at the curb opposite Dave's driveway, shooting down the side of the neighbor's house and out the back gate. I slipped beneath the hedgerows of old Mr. Carneggio's bungalow and lit across the lawn before his ancient poodle even had a chance to start yipping. I crossed the immaculate alley to my backyard, pushed through the ornate curls of the wrought iron gate, tripped over a teak chaise lounge, and almost landed in the pool. The house appeared empty.

The silence in the neighborhood unnerved me. I expected people to be hysterical and alarmed, bustling in and out of their houses, arms filled with swag they wanted to load into their minivans as they planned their escape to the questionable safety of the mountains. That's what Hollywood always showed in films based on alien invasions.

Instead, every house sat dark; the dim light illumining the windows was the blue glow of television sets.

Surprised to find the half-smoked joint still pinched tight between my thumb and forefinger, I raised the blunt to my lips and drew hard. Stale bitter air slurred down the paper tube. The cherry had burned to cold ash. I stashed the stub between my driver's license and the plastic card indicating my organs were available for harvesting. I'd always figured organ donation was a good guy kind of thing to do, just in case I crashed into one of the giant elms lining the neighborhood streets. I wondered, did being vaporized by aliens leave anything usable behind?

I darted in the rear door, catching the screen before the wood frame slapped back against the sill, and listened.

Dad's deep voice rumbled in an intense undertone further inside the house. I high-stepped down the hall and caught a glimpse of him standing beside the granite counter in the kitchen, his immaculate black suit slick and neat, not a wrinkle in sight. The regulation pair of dark sunglasses dangled from one hand. The other held his cell to his ear. He looked pretty much like he did every time he got called out for work.

He saw me. An expression of relief softened his hard features for a fraction of a second. With an abrupt gesture he ended the conversation, snapping the phone shut and palming the device into his suit pocket.

"You barely made it home in time." His voice had the familiar hard edge laced with an unfamiliar emotion.

That tiny hesitation hollowed out my lungs. Breath stolen, I took a step into the kitchen and opened my mouth to ask what-the-fuck but at that moment, the doorbell rang.

ALTERNATE ENDINGS

The sound echoed in the silence.

A foreboding rooted my feet to the tiled floor. I watched a strange expression cross Dad's face and I went cold inside.

His gaze caught me, the sort of straight-shooting stare that arrows past eyelids to pierce your soul in a search for connection. My throat closed up. Panic pushed adrenalin into my bloodstream. Heart muscle slammed against bone and cartilage, the hiccupping rhythm aggravated by an excess of alcohol and too little sleep.

"Dad?" I tried to stutter out a question but he grabbed one shoulder and pushed me aside, shoving something into my hand.

"Sacrifices are made every day, Jeremiah. This is my region. It makes sense I'd be a target. After your mother died, I told you the truth. Now you have to accept this may be the end for me. You know what to do, if that's the case. Remember, this is just part of the job. This isn't personal."

I stood with mouth gaping, a cartoon goldfish gasping for air.

He walked forward with his shoulders squared, his shoes gleaming and his hair perfect. Every movement was precise. Before he yanked open the heavy mahogany panel of the front door, his hand came up and he slipped the sunglasses into place.

I was proud of my dad, of how his shadowed profile looked all backlit by the blinding white light, and he faced the unknown like a bonafide Man in Black.

The shot didn't sound similar to the blast of a shotgun or the zing of a bullet. The attack, a sizzling burst of heat, blew my father across the room. He landed in a sprawl.

Light poured in to frame the humanoid shape in the doorway. The figure wore a silver spacesuit similar to the astronauts in those dumbass science fiction movies from the fifties. My fingers flexed, a sound leaked out from my lips, but still I couldn't move. The bulging misshapen head turned to peer at me.

I registered the movement of my arm in a detached way, the pulsing red device gripped in my hand seemed unconnected to the rest of me until a stream of energy poured from the tip. Sight and sound connected. The spaceman caught the discharge in the torso. The silver suit burst apart into shreds of colorful gristle and I smelled burnt flesh.

My knees wobbled but I jerked into motion and ran across the foyer.

Dad lay crumpled against the wall, one leg at a wrong angle, we splashes of blood shone on the taupe paint. Smoke drifted up in tendrils from the scorched wound in his chest. He grinned at me, his mouth lopsided and twisted from the pain, as he tried to speak.

I made more fish-faces, trying to figure out what to do first. My nose wrinkled from the stench but I couldn't think of anything but my dad being shot.

"Are you going to die?" I blurted out.

Dad gasped for a minute before he caught his breath and his inhalations evened out. "I don't think so." He coughed and grimaced, wafted away a curl of smoke with his hand. "Probably not."

I went down on my knees, not a graceful motion but it was better than collapsing into the remnants of the space dude. He reached over and slapped my thigh. "Sometimes this business gets messy, son. You did good."

ALTERNATE ENDINGS

Relieved, even if I worried he was lying to me; I tried not to see the goo making tracks down the exterior door. I wanted to whip out the half joint in my wallet and spark it up, but figured that might push dad right over the edge.

"Yeah, it reeks too."

He frowned at me, his brows furrowing forward. "That's all you have to say?"

Maybe it was the Jagermeister or the Jamaican Blue, but the suppressed angst of the last few hours burst out. "No, Dad! This entire thing is total bullshit! This was totally effing personal."

I flapped a hand toward the mess in the entry but my frantic emotional energy depleted like a spent balloon. I shrugged and dropped the funny pistol on the floor, slumping down to sit beside my old man.

He reached out with one hand and slap-punched my thigh, and started to laugh. He was still amused when the clean-up crew arrived.

3 CALL OF THE MUEZZIN

∽

FROM THE PINNACLE of Khufu's pyramid, Roland Wilkinson admired the view. There was nothing like this back home in his native England. The Giza plateau spread out in undulating sweeps until it disappeared into the horizon. The Nile River snaked a verdant line through the desolate landscape, the inundation still receding after the annual flood stage. Cairo lay beyond the ribbon of water. The distant jumble of geometric shapes looked oddly reminiscent of the London skyline, the towering minuets of the mosques spearing up like a forest of bristling peaks. The spiky rows reminded him of the musical notes of the requiem performed at Sophia's funeral mass. The shock of remembering his wife's death stole his breath for a second, but each time the pain faded, more so with every passing day.

Leaving behind the rainy cold of England for a winter in Egypt had been precisely the distraction he needed.

He'd postponed climbing the largest pyramid even though he'd been in residence most of the season. His dinner companions last evening had made the extraordinary claim that standing atop the monument of the long dead king allowed one to touch the vault of heaven. This morning Roland had wakened filled with curiosity to know if he would feel the same and so he'd set out to discover the truth.

Cairo sat far from where he now stood. He knew it was impossible to hear the muezzin calling the devout to evening prayer over such a great distance. Roland regretted not being able to discern the wavering ululation of cries as they echoed through the old part of the city. Strange as the call had at first been to his ears, he'd come to appreciate the uncertain music in the intonations. With eagerness he listened for the faithful being called to prayer, finding new appreciation in such literal acts.

The setting sun burned orange, casting the land into a feverish glow until it sank behind the hills. The intense heat of the day dissipated with surprising rapidity. A breeze kicked up and swept another of the incessant clouds of dust into a dervish of whirling energy.

Roland closed his eyes against the sting of the grit and cupped his hands together to protect his newest amusement. The tiny mechanical device warmed in his palms but he couldn't tell if the heat generated from the inner workings of the intricate machinery or from his body. The miniature face inside the two halves of the glass globe glowed from some luminescence within. He'd studied the piece through a magnifying lens but discovered nothing. At times he fancied the miniscule features underwent a transformation, appearing at one glance to be serious and thoughtful, and the next time to express whimsy or mischievousness.

Truly, it was a thing of remarkable craftsmanship. Roland found it an inspired piece of engineering even at the close of the nineteenth century when so many recent technological marvels had been conceived. He traced the exposed mechanisms through the transparent globe, imagining he had identified some of the same principals demonstrated in the finest of German clockworks. The exquisitely meshing gears and rotating elliptical spinning weights advanced a string of faceted black stones around the interior of the sphere. For what purpose, he'd no idea, but their movement fascinated him nonetheless.

The man who sold him the intriguing object knew even less. The native had been one of the many shabby illiterates who offered all manner of trinkets to visitors. The majority of the vendor's wares included the standard de rigueur miscellany of faience beads and shoddy faux replicas of priceless antiquities. Roland had ignored him altogether as he passed the narrow mastaba where the seller displayed his goods. The grimy hand thrust out to display the unusual piece. The frayed cuff of his blue and white striped galabeya, only a slight bit cleaner than the man himself, caught his attention. Roland's gaze latched on the gleaming smooth metal. The shiny glass sphere gleamed like a jewel. His step faltered. The seller leaned forward in a conspiratorial manner to offer him a closer inspection. The dragoman he'd hired to serve as his interpreter and guide for the afternoon, spouted forth a florid stream of Arabic words on his behalf.

The men haggled, as was the custom, but Roland would have purchased the beautiful novelty for the original asking price. It was a trifling expense to him. At that time he'd thought it an unusual watch piece. Accompanied by a glass of the Winter Palace Hotel's finest brandy, looked forward to examining the object at his leisure after dinner that evening.

Later, as he wandered the bazaar, Roland questioned the dragoman trailing on his heels. Ahmed happy to accommodate his wealthy patron, related the story of a Nubian oasis, hidden deep in the Sudan, far from the modern world. "It is said that a people reside deeper into the desert than a swift camel can reach. They commune with great flying monsters and live forever." The dragoman nodded his head for emphasis at the end of each pronouncement. According to the man, history was littered with stories of the amazing technology created by the descendants of the ancient pharaohs. He concluded by stating how the wisest and most devout of the believers had long ago vanished into the deserts of the western wilderness.

Roland found the stories entertaining. Rumors of lost oases persisted through the centuries. He knew the very idea was preposterous and yet the tales enlivened his imagination. He could offer no better explanation.

The people of Egypt, mired in their endless fascination with death, had distracted Roland from his own tragedy. The land provided an escape from the sorrowful remonstrance of well-intentioned friends, and although he missed his wife, distance created perspective. He understood that Sophia's loss had not been unexpected. The wasting illness ate her body until little more than a vague resemblance remained of the girl he'd married. She'd never regained consciousness during the final month.

Death freed them both.

The dust cloud passed. A cool breeze brought Roland back to the present. He opened his eyes, determined to shake off his melancholy. Fingers closing around the tiny treasure, he tucked it in his pocket while he enjoyed the view another moment. He needed to cross the platform to begin the lengthy descent. After night fell, he knew the process became even more treacherous. He swung around.

A native woman stood ten feet away.

Garbed in the typical dusty black robes, a semi-transparent veil obscured the lower half of her face. In the dying light her eyes sparkled as she stared at him.

A tremor of disquiet shivered up his spine. He'd lingered too long at the top of the pyramid. All the guides had departed. The teams of laughing men paid to whisk tourists up and down the sides of the colossal structure were absent. Far below Roland could see a contingency using the exposed stones as a gigantic staircase, the cluster of men swarming like a multi-armed god over the pale stones. The original slopes of the structure had been covered by hewn limestone sheets, each one hand-fitted into place to form a smooth exterior.

Drawing back, Roland tried to imagine how Khufu's massive tomb had appeared rearing up off the plain, gleaming white under the desert sun. Even now with the finished stones peeled away it was a glorious achievement.

Hand still tucked inside his jacket, he half bowed to the woman. His gaze never strayed from her regard until something sharp erupted from the trinket and stabbed his palm. Startled, he withdrew the object from his pocket. Legs and arms had sprouted from the bronze band that wrapped the middle circumference of the device. The petite robot climbed to its feet. Like a tiny soldier, it stood at attention on his outstretched palm. Rich red color glowed from within the glass. The creature's miniscule face showed features filled with longing. Its tiny bronze hands reached away from Roland, miniscule fingers clenching open and closed.

It wanted her.

Raising his gaze, Roland discovered the black-eyed woman now stood in front of him. Her head failed to reach the height of his chin but her eyes peered up at him, utterly fearless. A shudder passed through him. To his complete bafflement, a sense of recognition filled him up, like rainwater seeping into a spring cistern after an unexpected shower. With a gentle movement he thrust his hand forward and the tiny metal man danced across his lifeline, a portly gentleman with spindly appendages.

"Madam, I believe this creature recognizes you." He lowered his arm until the small figure stood between them.

A vibration thudding through the leather soles of his shoes made him dart a rapid look around, but the area remained deserted, save for the two of them. The sun had set. Now he would need to wait for moonrise before attempting the descent without the helpful guides to stabilize him as he dropped from one stone to the next. The woman's presence on the pyramid, unescorted at nightfall seemed unusual but perhaps that was why she had sought out his company.

A clunk sounded. He felt a release of air as though compressed steam issued from a slew of pipes. A heavy rumble echoed. He returned his attention to his companion in time to see a billow of dust rise up from the ground, haloing her black robes. She dropped the diaphanous veil. The shimmer of dying light altered her appearance. She smiled. Roland was lost in the whiteness of her teeth and the perfect shape of her lips. In the weeks that he'd navigated this antique land he'd never seen such superb dentition among his contemporaries, much less the native population who lived amid desperate poverty.

The woman raised a slender arm. The robot leaped from Roland's palm, wrapping its limbs around her dainty wrist. The glass glowed like a ruby and in that moment Roland realized the world was filled with new possibilities.

Similar to a curtain dropping across an operatic stage production, the air gave way behind the woman to reveal a monstrous vehicle. Its swollen shape was rounded at each end like one of the natural oddities Roland had seen during a visit to the British Maritime Museum. Constructed of gleaming metal and shining glass, the ship floated above the surface of the platform with no more effort than a whale floats through the ocean. Steam vented from appendages staggered along the side, pouring off like seawater streaming from a leviathan's spine. Smoke issued from dual stacks at the front and as he watched, a hatch swung open.

The native woman turned away, her black rob fluttering in the breeze.

Words tumbled out of Roland's mouth before caution or wisdom intruded. "Take me with you, please."

She paused to glance back over her shoulder. "Are you so willing to leave everything you know behind?"

Roland hesitated, considering the emptiness of his life. Then he nodded. Wherever the mighty ship was bound would prove a place unfamiliar to him. No one waited at home for him, not anymore. He had no pressing business anywhere. He waved a hand toward the plain, a long distance below, unconsciously encompassing the splendor of ancient Cairo in the gesture.

He offered a final entreaty. "But I have heard the muezzin call."

4 Adventure in the Caldera

Sam jacked up his injured leg and slammed the sole of his boot down on the egg. His muscles burned with the movement. The blue shell cracked at last. Two more blows shattered the thick rind, green yolk and slimy effluvia splattering up his pants leg. The nests lay under nearly every clump of greenery and the damn things weren't even edible. Their best stuntman had discovered that truth on the morning they exited the tunnel into the caldera. One bite of the scrambled mess swelled his tongue into a purpled black slug, choking him while a series of convulsive seizures caused him to suffocate.

The situation went downhill from there.

At first, the camera crew loved each minute of the gruesome footage.

In Sam's estimation, the entertainment industry was a truly fucked up business, but this current endeavor reached a whole new plateau of bend-over-and-take-it-hard. If any of them walked out of this antediluvian chuckhole alive, a sentiment fast earning a thumbs-down outlook, they'd all sworn to pocket one of those lizard eggs. Sam planned to treat his bastard of an agent to a special omelet. The fuckwit had sold him this tankard of bullshit, blowing smoke about his great return before the documentary camera.

Yeah, nix that idea.

Two of the three days they'd spent trudging around inside the extinct volcanic pit, had been squandered crawling back to the tunnel mouth, only to discover the passage blocked by a landslide. As usual, Sam was on point, leading the few men who'd demonstrated swift enough reflexes to survive the initial attacks.

It took zero effort to piece together what was happening. The muted thump of helicopter blades drew his face to the sky. The ghetto birds spiraled overhead like enormous vultures, shards of sunlight reflecting off the bristle of expensive of PS-Cam X35 lenses. Sam knew the meticulous bastards would record every moment of the expedition's sacrifice in the name of science on film. For primetime. Sam despised this new trend in reality television.

Especially since it might just make him a star again.

A babble of excited voices preceded the remainder of the expedition party. Half a dozen men burst through the vegetation, the gargantuan leaves of the ferns and other undergrowth shivering high overhead. They gathered in the clearing, their frightened eyes wide, chests heaving with exertion, shoulders weighted down under the surviving equipment. Most of the team's gear had been jettisoned when the killing started.

Flesh-eating foliage cost them two porters before they learned to identify and avoid the red-veined spiky leaves of the fatal plants. The wildlife offered another challenge. The dinosaurs were domestically-sized. Environmental constraints had created a closed ecosystem unable to accommodate megafauna, but as an experienced biologist, Sam knew size didn't alleviate risk. Even so, they'd all underestimated the ferocity of the nocturnal species.

The largest breed reached waist-high but demonstrated a voracious appetite and fierce speed. A pack swarmed their makeshift camp that first night, excising limbs with the rapacious snap of razor sharp teeth in jaws strong as hydraulic presses. Clack. Clack. Even the director gave a hand.

In less than twenty-four hours they'd lost three men. Everyone still alive had sustained injuries. The project was all but abandoned.

On top of that bullshit, a human predator had begun stalking the survivors with a silver blade. The killer slashed out from behind a tree and all but decapitated the boom operator, leaving them unable to record proper sound. A gut blow, delivered beside a twisted knot of root, eviscerated the lighting master. Their ability to shoot in less-than perfect light scrapped any chance of continuing, the gloom inside the jungle was too heavy, too green.

Now they'd circled back around to the start and were still shit-out-of-luck. Sam studied the raw rock face. He wondered if the side of the caldera was scalable. At age twenty-five he would have climbed up the cliff-face with his shirt torn wide and a thick hard-on displayed for the wide-angle focus on his crotch. Back then he'd been a female fan favorite. Now, at the low end of forty, he wasn't certain he'd make it to the top. He suspected the High-Indemnity-Release clause written into his contract had been optioned. That or his agent was tired of earning fifteen percent of nothing.

A scream jerked off in mid-cry. Sam paused to listen to the barrage of cursing that followed and decided it must be another burn from a razor fern. He had his own set of trophies to demonstrate how to handle the noxious plants. He thrust aside a frond, careful to avoid the gel-filled pustules that ran in a ridge on the underside of the branch. Two rows of blisters on his left forearm still burned from unwitting contact yesterday. His weakened thigh muscle cramped and the ragged wound from the bite mark continued to seep.

He stomped another egg and considered the pile of dusty rubble where the tunnel mouth had provided the sole access to the hidden valley. A desperate climb up the steep loose scree of the escarpment would make a good camera shot and though he was no hero, he considered it as an option. Going down hard got the movers and shakers buzzing in Hollywood.

Sam crushed the last egg in the nest and moved back into the sunlight. He ignored one of the tiny blue lizard-like creatures when it darted across his path. The stinging bites of the small ones proved more a nuisance than a real danger unless they swarmed. The larger sleek black-and-green striped biters were fast bastards. One of those had gotten his leg. He'd seen the yellow eyes peering from beneath the dense undergrowth and clued in to the fact the reptiles ate eggs. He figured removing the available food source might buy them some time.

ALTERNATE ENDINGS

The constant churn of dust and noise wore on Sam's sinuses and his nerves. He flipped off the hovering helicopters without glancing up, hoping every ultra-zoom lens showed the dried blood caked under his fingernails.

He joined Josh in studying the collapsed cliff face. The boy's hands were marked with scratches and bound with dirtied bandages in a fruitless effort to stave off infection. They were all goners, when you considered the long-term. Germs, gangrene, dinosaur-snack...there wasn't much difference. The end result worked out the same. Eyes lingering on the crusty brown rag that marked where the boy's left little finger used to be, Sam's jaw tightened. Josh had been one of the lucky guys, he hadn't lost anything critical. He liked the kid. A college drop-out, the boy was a genius if you put a camera in his hands. This had been his first big break. His role in the endeavor had improved as each crew member's loss meant an instant promotion.

Josh dragged dirty fingers through his tousled black curls and winced. "The director is dead."

So much for the promotions.

If they set up a makeshift camp at the top of the slope they'd at least have more visibility. He debated whether it was better to see death coming for you on the hoof, or just feel the gnashing teeth pierce your chest, when Josh said something that caught his attention.

"Say again."

"I got a good look at the killer. It's a man with red hair. He's swinging this huge blade around."

Sam glowered. "Small guy? Green eyes and a scar on his chin?"

Josh's mouth dropped open and he nodded.

Sam swore. "I told my motherfucking agent I wouldn't work with Brad Doulton again." He lurched into motion, leaving Josh to stumble along in his wake. "He and I worked together on that disastrous Amazon series, five years ago." Sam spat the words over his shoulder as he charged toward the bedraggled film crew huddled in a circle. "Get up you lazy bastards." Sam kicked the boot of the man nearest him and bared his teeth in a grin. He pointed at the circling helicopters. "We've got a primetime rating in a hot new serial or they wouldn't still be filming."

In an instant, the men became alert, their eyes shooting skyward. They climbed to their feet, swaying and staggering, renewed energy flushing through wasted limbs.

Josh grabbed one of the camera straps and hoisted the equipment to his shoulder. "What's the shoot?"

"We're giving them what they want. Our murderous friend is going to be fed to the dinosaurs in front of the cameras. Then we climb to safety."

Josh's mouth gaped and caught Sam's attention.

"Let me guess, Josh, you're so green you failed to demand a Sudden-Death-Exemption clause in your contract?"

The boy's face colored a deep red.

Sam slapped a hand over the kid's narrow shoulder. Hope burgeoned in his chest. They had a chance to turn this around and come out on top. Excitement burned through him. He'd take Josh all the way up with him. He was back in the game.

Daylight brought the helicopters.

Sam flipped his middle finger at the shiny CNN chopper. Damn news vultures would replay the image for days. The studio and the network had sold them down the river. Years of experience in show biz had taught him the best way to survive a season, was to win viewers. If they could get the public rooting for the surviving members of the documentary film crew, they'd have a better chance of climbing out of this caldera while they still had the body parts to do so.

Americans love the underdog.

Hunger pangs twisted his shrunken stomach. This was their second morning without food. The stream water hadn't killed them but Sam imagined the slow progress of diatoms and microbes infesting the interior working of his body, breaking down and analyzing his internal defense systems, seeking out yet another way to immobilize him.

The environment would kill them, assuming the dinosaurs didn't take them down first. The trek through the caldera introduced dozens of extinct species. If it weren't for biological downsizing due to the environmental constraints, they'd already have been reptile snacks. The more aggressive examples stalked human-sized prey with ease.

At least they usually heard the big ones coming.

Sam's old nemesis offered an additional twist to the survival challenge. The men had taken to calling the knife-wielding slasher, Brad-the-Blade. He waited somewhere nearby, anticipating his next kill.

Making the assumption that fire was a universal deterrent, Sam instructed the others to gather wood. The able-bodied began to heave rocks into a rough fortress along the base of the cliff. With solid stone at their backs, sturdy walls on both sides, and a firepit at the entrance, they might make it through another day.

The specter of starvation already dodging his heels, Sam was desperate. He needed a solution. A real one. He drew a hard line at cannibalism.

After considering the possibility of bringing down one of the omnipresent helicopters, he decided the lack of suitable tools would hamper any plan. A crash might not bring rescue, but the plot twist would offer opportunistic filming. Taking out a chopper filled with studio bigwigs could rewrite the script and guarantee a ratings boost. Win-win. He chewed on that thought for a moment and tucked it away in the back of his mind for later evaluation.

In all likelihood, he'd earned more money in the last four days than during the entire length of his career. Guess that was one benefit of being stalked by a killer herpetologist in a dinosaur-infested volcanic cinder cone. This story guaranteed to get him laid if he survived.

Sam pointed at the camera man. "What haven't I thought of?"

Josh sat across from him, back-to-back with one of the surviving crewmen. The boy twitched and jerked, made nervous by the skittering in the undergrowth, every new sound presaging another dinosaur attack in his sensory oversaturated mind.

Once the sun set, the thumping sounds of the helicopters dissipated for the evening. Even with heat-recognition technology, all the viewers could hope to see were red blurs. Cold-blooded dinosaurs didn't register. Sam wondered how long a human limb would glow under the night-vision sensors once a creature snapped it off his body.

Their third night in the caldera was the most comfortable so far. They'd managed to form a secure nest against the cliff by piling up rocks to create a miniature box canyon. A fire at the mouth of the room kept the dinosaurs at bay. So far nothing had dropped down the cliff-face but Sam figured it was only a matter of time before something toothy, poisonous, or both, did. He fed a stick to the flames and returned to puzzling out why his agent had set him up for this job. Sure, his career had gone stale. The Amazonian debacle had blacklisted him from legitimate documentary endeavors. The few offers he received were natty spots in dubious research expeditions, like this one. Back in his glory days, this project would have been an instantaneous reject. Even after he'd read the contract and knew he was going to take the role, he'd still felt compelled to make a scene.

Dinosaurs in the modern day, he'd jeered back with a dismissive curse, tossing the envelope on the coffee table. Photographs had spilled out, flooding over the edge of the glass top like an old fashioned film strip, piling up around his feet. Dinosaurs. They were god-awful realistic-looking monstrous creatures, for all their small stature. Dredged up from a half-forgotten memory in an evolutionary biology class, came the recognition of the background flora, ferns and broadleaf trees long gone extinct.

Sam's senses had buzzed with the impossible.

His body jumped forward before his mind finished making the connection. He scooped up the pile and studied each glossy photo while his agent picked up the phone and made arrangements. The bastard even accepted the Sudden-Death-Exemption clause in Sam's contract with a solemn expression. Now Sam was certain his High-Indemnity-Release rider had been optioned and his slimy personal representative stood to make a lot of profit off his on-screen death. At least the bastard would have to share it with Sam's ex-wife since he'd never gotten around to striking Vicki's name off his beneficiary list. That fact gave him a perverse pleasure now.

One of the crew moaned in his sleep, twitching with the pain of his injuries. Deprivation and hunger, exposure and infection all took a toll on the survivors. The sands had almost run out of the hourglass.

Sam blamed Brad Doulton for screwing up his life. The greedy shit had upstaged him in the past and left him looking like an imbecile. Sam's marketability factor had plummeted. He was determined that would never happen again, even if he had to take drastic measures. He slept, waking before dawn to check the fire. He looked at his watch. They'd made it to day four.

Today would be the tipping point.

With unanimous agreement, the survivors of the expedition voted to feed Brad to the cameras. The plan was a simple bait and switch. Josh offered himself up as the lure, and since the boy was the youngest and least-injured of the crew, Sam agreed. The idea worked like a choreographed dance sequence, the cocky killer waltzed into their makeshift camp, slashing left and right with a cackle of mad laughter.

Sam leaped from beneath one of the ferns, but he was too slow to stop Brad from flexing his bicep and making the blade arc down to bite deep into the waist of the assistant director. He surged forward and pierced Brad's ribcage with the stick he'd spent an hour sharpening. The end of the spear, coated thick with poisonous slime from one of the dinosaur eggs, ripped through muscle and tissue. Brad dropped the knife to clutch at the injury.

ALTERNATE ENDINGS

A river of petite reptilian forms flooded out from under the striated ferns and flowed across the bare expanse. Concerned, Sam spied them and turned to watch. Whatever the tiny predators fled from would also eat humans. He shouted a warning just as pandemonium erupted.

The surrounding foliage separated and a slick green hide muscled into view. Speckled with orange dots and streaked with silver smears, the sauropod lumbered in his path on stumpy legs. Sam dove to one side. He knew this dinosaur ate plants but they had also seen it snacking on the miniature raptors.

Seeing his adversary stumbling away, Sam snatched up the blade and bolted after the man responsible for ruining his professional career.

The sauropod blundered behind the agile lizards, snapping its beaklike snout. It stopped dead at the sight of Brad, myopic eyes narrowing until it issued a snort and with a dismissive air, turned and trotted away.

Brad lunged toward the line of greenery, one arm tucked against his bleeding side.

Sam sprinted forward, intent on following, but the trees in front of him blew apart. A Tyrannosaurus Rex stomped out of the jungle.

Helicopters swarmed overhead. The whump of blades churned up dust and debris. The choppers hovered dangerously close, vying for the tightest close-up. Dozens of lenses aimed at the sweat beaded on wrinkled foreheads and focused on bloody gashed wounds.

Rapacious mouth agape, rows of teeth gleamed in the sun. The T-Rex advanced. Reduced in scale but not ferocity, the giant lizard's alert eyes tracked the screaming men. The massive jaws swiveled from one potential target to another. The dinosaur ignored the thump of blades and with a sudden intensity, fixated on Brad's red hair. The color of blood, his head bobbing in a fiery dance a perfect six feet off the ground, the man's skull became a beacon to the beast.

Sam didn't think he imagined the cheers erupting inside the hovering crafts.

Sound booms lowered like an inverted sea of kelp stalks, intent on capturing every growl and snarl from the arena below. Snapping lenses and digital streams documented each second of the man's final moments.

The bite caught Brad's torso. Six inch incisors pierced flesh and collapsed his lungs. Jaws stronger than hydraulic rams splintered his ribs. Not a whimper escaped the man.

The rest of them dove for cover.

The tyrannosaur's muscles rippled as she shook Brad's body.

His arms and legs flailed loose like a child's cloth doll. She tossed her trophy and his corpse fell, a sack of brittle sticks. The dinosaur dove on her prey and clamped the headless form between her steely jaws. With a shudder of movement and a swipe of her monstrous tail, she disappeared into the gloom.

Raucous glee leaked down from the filming network affiliates.

Josh staggered up beside Sam. "Don't you just love dinosaurs?" A smile curved his mouth.

They found the boom operator face down on the trail, his throat slashed. Small predators feasted at both sides of the gaping wound. A second body, the onsite studio representative, lay sprawled at the edge of a nest beneath the ferns.

Fragments of crushed blue shell littered the ground around him. The voracious appetites of the jungle denizens made burying the dead unnecessary, so they left the bodies.

Pleased with the success of their plan so far, Sam calculated their prospects for survival had increased a significant jump with Brad's demise but then plummeted with proof of the tyrannosaur's existence.

Now, the survivors numbered four. All were wounded, one mortally. Beneath the watchful scrutiny of the choppers they retreated to the meager shelter and crawled inside.

The helicopters departed at midday, leaving behind an unnerving silence.

Brad's murderous blade hung from Sam's belt now. He and Josh took turns feeding the fire, sleeping as much as possible. In a few hours it would be Friday. They were nearly out of time. Sam shifted his leg and winced. The injury had worsened, the infection seeping clear red-streaked fluid. An occasional hard nugget of pus forced its way to the surface and left a hole. The rags he used to bind the jagged slice stank of putrefaction.

He inventoried the rest of their injuries.

Josh had lost a little finger to one of the biters and part of an ear to Brad's lethal blade. The sound guy was in pretty good shape, except for a trio of seeping gashes in one forearm. The assistant director breathed with a wet rattle, every inhalation a labor for his perforated chest. Nobody thought he'd last out the day. They all sported chemical burn trails on their arms from the nasty pustules beneath the fern fronds.

Sam wondered if the poisonous slime from the eggs had burned through Brad's bloodstream. He hoped it scorched like acid. That would be primal. He wanted the bastard to have felt every inch of canine pierce his chest. The cameras ate up the action, the helicopters flying low for focused head shots, desperate to capture the fight in multicolor detail. He figured the ghoulish voyeurs would return at first light, anxious to know if anyone survived the night. It worried him that they'd left the day before and not returned. It made Sam wonder what other surprises lay in store.

The assistant director had extracted a promise from each of them, insisting they throw him out as fodder when he became insensible. "They'll pay a bonus if I'm still kicking and screaming." He said between wet inhalations.

They knew he was right. The indignity of being eaten alive would option the Final-Moment clause in his contract and earn his widow the money to put all three kids through college. That had to count for something.

Sam hated reality television even more now that he found himself starring in what was no doubt the hottest new series. His thoughts jerked to a stop. *Friday.* Could it be showdown time already? Were they destined for the shortest season in Hollywood history? They needed a reversal in the story, a dramatic extension.

Now was the moment to play that card.

"Why would the studio invest so much time and effort into a production run that spanned a single week?" Sam voiced his skepticism aloud.

His words woke the others.

Josh latched on to his reasoning and started to chatter, excited words flooding out of his mouth. "We've been prolonging the end and the network has extended the viewing platform. At least one of us has to survive a while longer for a ratings climax."

Sam nodded.

The assistant director shifted on to his side, gasping for air, face grey and blotchy.

Everyone waited until his breathing eased enough for him to speak.

"There has to be a cache of food and medicine, maybe even a secure shelter somewhere so we have a fighting chance of staying alive, but there'll be a ticking clock. Something will force us back outside." He ran out of breath again.

The others looked at each other.

The sound guy fed more wood to the fire. "We trekked halfway across the valley. If anything is hidden out there, how do we find it?"

"Maybe we were supposed to confront Brad?" Josh said in a doubtful tone. He turned to Sam. "Even if they had automatic cameras planted inside the structure and on the exterior, they wouldn't be able to film us getting back through the jungle. If I was in charge of the shoot, I'd want to record every angle and bite." He scratched the skin above the stump of his missing finger.

The proverbial light bulb sparked over Sam's head. He raised his face to look up the sheer side of the cliff. The overhanging lip swelled out in a bulge, hundreds of feet above their heads.

The others could see he'd thought of something.

Josh's voice wavered but he spoke aloud everyone's thoughts. "The best exposure is on the high ground. They've milked what they can from the jungle and the dinosaurs.

Now they want to force us to go head-to-head against each other."

The sound guy didn't even look up. "It isn't possible to scale that fucking cliff."

"Just feed me to the biters. I can't sit up, anymore." The assistant director's bitter humor left a potent silence.

Sam frowned. There had to be a way up the cliff, a switchback trail or winding passage that would allow them, even in crappy physical condition to climb out of the caldera.

He waited till first light and then skirted the fire, telling the others to stay put. A hundred yards past the collapsed tunnel entrance he found the narrow declivity between two rocks but the path disappeared into a thick rock fall. If more crew members had survived they might have been able to dig their way through the blockage. With only three of them even mobile, this was an unbeatable obstacle. He back-tracked, eyes scanning the undergrowth, ears listening for the telltale rustle of a predator.

In less than an hour the sky would lighten and the cameras return. For the first time in his professional career Sam wanted to blow a scene. They'd set him up good, but if anyone could still turn this around, somehow it must be him. He'd help the remaining survivors escape the caldera and win. The choppers and executives would all look like fools. He'd go home victorious, the hero of the hour, and the survivor of the studio sacrifice.

Killing his agent was the first priority when he got back to Los Angeles.

Sam returned to the shelter and dozed until the sun had inched far enough across the sky to brighten the deep ravine.

ALTERNATE ENDINGS

A rhythmic whump punctured the silence and interrupted their rest, but the sound of a single helicopter brought them all outside, even the assistant director who clutched his abdomen in pain and had to be half-carried around the firepit.

The studio insignia painted on the panels of the small craft was instantly recognized.

Without warning a wooden crate tumbled out the side door. Suspended by cable until the container was three yards from the ground, the latch released and the crate hit hard and cracked open. Brightly colored boxes spilled out, followed by what looked like camping equipment and the steel-blue shine of weapons.

The men stared at the array of objects, puzzled.

Josh pointed at a pile of packages. "Are those toaster pastries and powdered drink mixes?"

Sam snorted out a laugh and gave the group a thumbs-up. "Congratulations are in order, gentlemen. We have official product endorsements. That means we've been renewed for another season."

The crash of a second and a third container drowned out the cheers."

5 Find Yourself in Maui

⁓

H O'OPONO HAD BEEN born on Maui and he never tired of admiring her beauty and grace. Here in the sacred valley is where he felt closest to the ancient ones. The shadows in the crevasse lengthened as the sun slipped below the horizon and with unexpected suddenness Iao was flung into darkness.

Behind him the malahini stood wide-eyed on the viewing platform, drinking in the dazzling allure of this holy place. The crowd was small and intimate, just like the council had agreed. He had been patient and let the curious tourists come to him, asking him to deliver a real Hawaiian experience. Tonight they would get what they wished for, a genuine taste of the old ways. Power swirled through the air, a current of sentient breath seeking out and finding his offering, pleased to discover the four couples readied for sacrifice and prepared to augment the volcano.

He pushed aside the canvas flap of the pavilion, ducked inside and found Kanunu kneeling before the altar. He waited in respectful silence while she arranged items with precise movements. Beside a burning candle she placed fresh breadfruit against the curve of a pink and white pu shell. A strand of dark kakui nuts tangled with a lei made of ti leaves, draped around a bundle of taro. All of the items rested atop the coil of palm fiber cordage he'd spent hours twining into a taut rope.

When she finished her ministrations he prompted her in a soft voice. "The guests wait, Kanunu."

She nestled the coconut bowl filled with ohelo and akala berries into the array and rose to her full five foot height. "I have prepared to share the joy that is ancient Hawai'i."

A shrug slipped off his unbuttoned shirt and Ho'opono dropped the garment as he preceded the sister of his father back outside to the gathering. He drew the curious attention of the tourists by contracting the pectoral muscles of his brown torso and making the intricate black tattoos dance. He endured the greedy strength of their gazes as they inspected the ancient patterns sweeping down his shoulders and across his chest to where they ended at the bony prominences of his ribs. Desire flared in the eyes of several, but not recognition or comprehension. For those who could read the symbolism, like the elders in the village who had taught him, the heavy patterns portrayed his high status and reflected the same kin markings that also graced Kanunu's forearms and the backs of her hands.

Ho'opono paused near the break-away rail and watched the haoles go still, their absorption shifting to Kanunu as they became captivated by her beauty. Descended from the first bloodline, older than the kingdoms, predating the territorial governance and prior to statehood, her regal bearing and graceful steps stole their gasps. The simple crown of maile leaves entranced the viewers, the brilliant pearl crescent of her smile caused each to forget her thin blouse and cotton skirt had been purchased from the local Wal-Mart.

The narrow rope bridge rippled in the late evening breeze, the sole connective link between the flanks of the Pu'u Kukui Crater and their position atop the pinnacle of basalt thousands of feet above the Iao Valley floor.

Contrasts met and embraced in this locus, fused in a blending of old and new.

When Kanunu raised her arms, the silence was complete.

Ho'opono sensed the moment the past surged forward to claim the present. Tonight he would witness Maui take another step toward becoming whole.

Unlike the flame twirlers and elaborate staged luau dinner shows that had been popularized around the islands, Ho'opono's village offered a *traditional* experience. The hungry haoles yearned for a connection to the raw spirit of the archipelago. He and Kanunu presented a premiere service to fulfill that desire.

The family guardians, the na 'aumākua, had been generous, providing plentiful offerings to feed the hungry na 'unihipili who gathered beside the stream. Here the earliest and most venerated chiefs lay sequestered in hidden abodes.

The correct honoring of those leaders was of equal importance in reviving the collective memory of the people.

The song, rooted deep within Ho'opono, climbed through his interior until the words spilled from his mouth in a rich sonorous utterance that brought the surf rushing up the faraway beach. The chanted cadence rose and fell in undulating waves of sound. He began to move, the slap of his soles a staccato accompaniment, the melody carrying his prayers into the clouds.

Flame burst from Kanunu's palm. She raised her hand high so the plume stretched upward, reaching for the first stars after nightfall.

He saw her lips move and knew she had invoked the names of the lava beings. He sensed the answering tremors from the volcanic terrain.

There were no wary glances directed at one another, or expressions indicating unease, from those present. Elation swelled and overflowed Ho'opono when each visitor climbed to their feet and began to sway. His voice grew stronger. The rhythm of his intonations wove together elements of air and wind with water and sea, and bound the living of the land with the dead of the soil.

Soon now, the ground would shake and the mountain split open, the maw of the crater stretch wide to swallow the offerings in Kuka 'emoku, the sacred site of the stone spear.

The Fire Gods, anxious to gather their special gifts close, would marvel at the color of the flame-haired woman. They would enfold the man with the big laugh and loud aloha, with joyful arms, loving each. One-by-one they would endear their hearts and lives to the ancestors. The people together could at last become 'ohana, the single lineage, united.

ALTERNATE ENDINGS

"Dance. Follow the flame." Kanunu sang, her body rolling and hips flowing, hands waving the story of the world into existence.

The guests moved en masse. Swaying and twisting, arms curved in graceful arches above their heads, chanting and stamping their bare feet, they advanced. They smiled and reached for the heat, welcomed the rush of exhilaration brought into being by the ancient rite. Their hearts crackled with the energy of life.

In a final fluid bow Kanunu allowed the blaze to lick from her fingers and break free into the sky. The fire cascaded, plummeting into blackness, a golden rivulet of flickering light.

One at a time, the tourists stepped through the gap into the empty abyss.

The night took them singly. Silently.

Ho'opono knew envy. He longed to experience such devotion, to be consumed and devoured by the essence of the earth. To lie down in the cool soil and let the tides pull at his bones, to nourish the generations to come, and to understand everything and know all.

Kanunu's warm hand touched his cheek, wiped away the tears with her fingers, and calmed him. "It is a great gift we have shared."

He blinked back another wave of emotion when she lifted the lei of bright yellow and orange blossoms over his head and lowered the fragrant blooms on his shoulders. He inhaled the lingering scent of lava, wrinkled his nose as the pungent odor tickled his nostrils.

A quick glance showed eight sets of sandals and loafers tucked beneath the benches. He accepted the plastic trash bag and with solemn features he collected the footwear, slinging the sack over his shoulder when he had finished. He'd drop them at the charity store in the morning, just as he'd done with the last batch. Everyone knew that tourists often forgot personal belongings. The staff never wondered why they donated so many shoes.

6   Blind Mary

I OPEN SLEEP-CRUSTED eyes and discover Aunt Mary sitting across from me. I blink but she's still there so I close my eyelids and inhale a deep breath. The room smells funny. Tobacco smoke and sweat are familiar enough, but there's something more, like grease and soot. Then the sensation of movement from the surface beneath me registers. I spread my eyes wide. Mary continues to stare at me, the lenses of her small round spectacles reflecting the shine from the lantern affixed to the wall behind her shoulder. It's impossible to know if she is aware of the scrutiny.

A new thought penetrates my disjointed senses. The light emanates from an oil lamp. I shift on the hard bench and push into a sitting position, head aching like the time I took a double-dose of cold medicine. I peer at the wall. Yep, a flame flickers inside the glass globe. Unreal.

I check if Mary is still there. She is. That fact surprises me, but I'm distracted by a roil of alarm because I realize the seat beneath me is *in motion.*

I'm aboard a train.

The sway of the rail car makes Mary's torso undulate. The movement reminds me of the belly dancer I watched in a YouTube video last week but the resemblance ends there. I frown at the quantity of fabric making up the skirt of her dress. Nobody wears ankle length dresses. Even the Amish and Mennonite families we study in social science class don't wear such stuffy clothes. On the upside, the soft rose hue brings to mind the blooms in mom's flower garden.

I wrap my hands over the edge of the seat and enjoy the stability. Why am I on a train in the company of my mother's reclusive and mysterious sister? I should be in algebra class, suffering through my sophomore year of high school, trying to work up the nerve to talk to a girl just like all the other boys my age. I glance around but there are no other passengers.

Mary sits still, swaying with the gentle motion of the car. The strong contrast of black hair and pale skin compliments her narrow face and smooth complexion.

During my life she's come and gone without providing notice of arrival or departure. She simply walks up the steps to the porch, reaches out and grasps the brass knob polished by three generations of our family, and opens the door.

Few people even realize she's blind. To all appearances the lack of eyesight matters little in her life.

ALTERNATE ENDINGS

A swell of steam bursts with a wet hiss from the locomotive somewhere up ahead of the passenger car where we sit. If not for that incongruous note, it might be a normal day.

Not.

"What happened?" My voice cracks even though I will it to be steady.

The almost imperceptible tightening of Mary's mouth indicates she finds my fear amusing. She leans forward and lays long fingers on my forearm.

"Calm yourself, Joseph."

I don't understand what the hell that is supposed to mean. Mary enjoys being a cipher and I'm damn proud to remember the word from last week's English class. Mrs. Rubenstein's goal this year is to force us to improve our vocabulary.

I clear my throat, a dry hacking sound, and try again. "Where are we?"

Mary cocks her head to one side, studying my face, except I know she can't see.

The image throws me back in memory to the first time I met her, the night my older sister Amelia went missing. Even at ten years of age, I recognize Mary for a freak. Mom's lone sibling has never visited and her arrival is unexpected but Mother falls unhesitating into her outstretched arms, wailing and tearful. I avoid them both in the mad disarray of unfolding events.

There is a sense that my aunt is always near at hand, just out of visual range, compelling me to wonder if it is I who is without vision. I find her intense concentrated stare unnerving, like she focuses through those milky white eyes and finds me somehow wanting.

Both she and my uncle are blind, but no one ever notices she lacks sight. Occasionally I worry that whatever made their vision go wrong, might be catching.

Mary left after a week. She walked out the front door, down the stairs, and disappeared into the night.

The police had also vanished by then. The phone calls from neighbors and friends had trickled to a halt. Neither of my parents appeared worried anymore, at least not about finding my missing sister. That puzzled me. When I demand to know why they are no longer crying, Uncle Bart sends me to my room. He's never ordered me to do anything. I go.

The blurred half-remembered scenes grow hazy in my mind. I veer off that route down memory lane.

Mary reappeared yesterday, materializing out of nowhere, like one of those disembodied spirits in a video game except she's made of flesh and blood.

One second I'm staring out the big window of the front parlor at the empty street and the next she's stepping onto the top step. It was like she emerged straight from the ether of the summer night and moved during the fraction of a second when I blinked.

She grips a single bag in one hand and carries a shawl slung over the opposite arm. The visual is similar to old photographs of southern refugees in the aftermath of the War Between the States. History is one of my favorite subjects.

Tiny round purple lenses hide her sightless eyes, but she has none of the awkward mannerisms Uncle Bart displays. Like a normal blind person, he waddles down the halls of our creaky house, fingers trailing the faded wallpaper, his cane tapping out a muted rhythm on the tiles. Mary walks with grace, her lean figure moves like a dancer. She carries no stick to aid her. Her fingertips do not trace any surface. She does not need touch for identification. Mary never ages.

Sometimes I think she does have sight even though the vacant eyes behind the glasses are filled with emptiness. My heart gives a nervous jump every time she touches me.

I shiver now and she withdraws the hand.

The rocking of the train is a more familiar motion, but my perception of unreality grows stronger with every glance around. Polished wood gleams. A carpeted path leads down the center aisle of the passenger car, stretching from one end of the car to the opposite door. The mirror-bright windows reflect the passing countryside, an endless vista of grassy prairie. Nothing makes any sense to me.

I try to understand how this came about. Despite my uncertain feelings toward my aunt, I am grateful for her presence now. I remember Mary departing the house this morning and I followed.

Curious about her method of travel, I anticipate a waiting taxi and slip out the door behind her. I can be quiet when I need to be, one of the few virtues of being small for my age. I recall the latch clicking shut, the whoosh of sound, and a disorientation lasting a full minute. The sensation lingers like the woozy effects of the shot of bourbon I sneak behind the summer house every Labor Day barbecue.

Then the nausea and chills erupt.

A whistle-blast sounds. The piercing noise spikes through my head. I cringe and blink, slap both hands over my ears.

The effect is like coming awake after an afternoon nap, drowsy with dreams, into a full-blown panic attack. In the month after my sister Amelia disappeared, I felt the same way every time someone left the house.

I really am sitting inside a railcar, the wooden bench hard beneath my ass. Wood smoke and the stench of sweat permeate the air. I lower my hands to touch the rough wool trousers encasing my legs. Sturdy boots stud my feet. They're heavy when I pick up my right foot and let it drop. The heel makes a solid clunk against the plank floor. A collarless shirt buttons down my chest.

I scuff palms down my thighs, register the feel of muscles retracting, and fight the sense of rightness.

"Where are we?" I ask again, no longer worrying if the note of panic is evident in my cracking voice. I might very well inquire *when we are* because by the look of things, *here* appears to be the nineteenth century.

Don't think about that.

A breath of laughter slides out from between Aunt Mary's thin lips. "We've come to collect your sister."

I freeze. Something, maybe a wild hope, catches in my throat.

Amelia, six years older than me, went missing at sixteen. I am now that age and an equal number of birthdays have passed. The numerical confluence distracts my frazzled brain for a moment with a pattern that must have meaning.

Something is very wrong. Maybe I'm experiencing a psychotic episode.

I study Mary's expressionless face and ignore the bizarre evidence of time and place all around me. It takes effort to push the words out of my mouth but years of counseling from school therapists reinforce my ability to speak the truth I don't believe.

"Amelia's gone. We must accept that and get on with our lives."

ALTERNATE ENDINGS

It's the same statement I've repeated on hundreds of occasions and heard many times more. The speech is the litany of social workers, liaison officers from the local police department, and concerned neighbors. The phrases have become my own personal mantra when questioned by a well-meaning adult. Each helpful reverberation confirms the inevitable conclusion.

Nobody ever suggests Amelia ran away from home. That always bothers me, like someone knows that isn't an option, which means they know something the rest of us don't. I reject the idea my sister is a runaway but I want some person, anyone, to think it's a possibility.

Mary smiles, a gentle sweep of her lips that curves in an amused arc. She holds out a rectangle of paper toward me.

I lean forward so I can grasp the offering and catch sight of myself in her violet-tinted glasses, my reflection distorted. Suppressing a shiver, I take the photograph, turn it around and glance down.

An icy trail inches up my spine.

"Amelia has been found." Mary says.

The picture is old, the edges frayed and cracked, because it was taken more than a century ago. It displays a trio of people.

We three.

I recognize myself, seated in a chair with my back to the photographer, a traveling hat atop my blonde head. Amelia perches on the right, at my side, her dark hair twisted up in a grown-up style. She is older and prettier and looks so much like our mother. Mary stands on the opposite, her intense gaze, even behind the concealing spectacles, challenges the camera. One hand grasps a broom as if the picture-taking has interrupted her in the act of sweeping the floor.

The bizarre image sparks an association of witchery, a surrealistic tableau that would appeal to artists in the first half of the twentieth century. Just now, I consider anything possible.

I whisper Amelia's name, hear the dazed echo of pain in my voice. I miss my sister and want to believe she might come home.

Mary flicks her fingers in my direction and plucks the picture from my hand. "We're approaching the station. Put on your hat and coat. You will make a good impression."

I glance down and find both the coat and the hat from the photograph, beside me on the seat. Once again I experience the unnerving sensation that I lack vision.

The train slows.

The whistle shrieks. The squeal of iron wheels scrape against the track. The sounds drown out everything else. I grab the bench when the car lurches and momentum pulls me forward.

Trees flash past the window and then the fronts of buildings, like still images in an old photo album, or snapshots from the National Archives.

I glimpse a hand-painted sign suspended from iron hooks. The wooden plank features a single word I take to be the name of the town. A moment later the train shudders to a standstill. We've arrived at the station in Eternity.

A plume of steam obscures my view of the platform.

Unsteady, I climb to my feet. The soles of my boots sit familiar on the floor, an unaccountable sensation. The texture of the black coat, as I slide my arms into the sleeves, is comforting. I feel like I've come home after a long journey.

Mary waits at the sliding door with one hand outstretched. "Hurry along, Joseph. We must make our appointment."

I take a step forward, wrap my fingers around hers and let a blind woman lead me into the past.

The smells strike me first.

Sweet pungent sagebrush from the prairies mixes with fresh horse droppings, and the unaccountable stench of garbage composting outside the rear doors of every building is pervasive. Old mud cakes everything. Muddy splashes arc up the sides of each business that comes in to view while we cross the platform. The road in front of the depot features ruts so deep I can track back to where wagons have been abandoned on the outskirts of town and people walk in to complete their shopping.

Never a fan of old westerns, I am caught in a wakeful nightmare.

Mary pulls me along. The heels of her shoes ring on the plank sidewalk. Her sense of urgency galvanizes me into action. Impending peril emanates from her hurried motions.

I find my footing forging across the dirt lanes. The ground squeezes up around my boots, the hardened crust sun-dried but the layers beneath still soft with moisture. I can't imagine the deluge necessary to create such a morass.

Even with twenty/twenty vision I struggle to cross the ruts and keep up with Mary's frenetic pace. She never loosens her hold on my sleeve, fingers locked over my wrist like an iron manacle.

"When we arrive at our destination, you must not react as if you recognize your sister. We're going to pose for the man taking the picture. Simple enough, right? Afterwards, we'll depart. Amelia will accompany us to the door. When you hear the crack of thunder there is only a matter of seconds to clasp hands. Grab Amelia in a tight grip and shut your eyes, wait for the flash of light and then leap forward like you were jumping off the overpass."

My mind seizes on the one inconsequential part of the delivered instructions. Somehow Mary knows Amelia taught me to close my eyes before leaping off the local bridge into the deep rushing waters of Cumberland Creek.

At this point I'm operating on instinct and following orders. If a train ride and a crazy dash through mucky streets can bring my sister back, I'm game. If fate will send us home together and restore the cracked vessel of my family into a pitcher that holds water; well, there isn't much I wouldn't attempt.

No one pays us any attention. The people we pass shift their eyes away from our presence, not that they can't see us, but more like they are committed to not making a connection.

My senses say this is all happening, which means I am really here. Nevermind that this town looks like a vintage western movie set from Lone Pine. The sights and sounds convince me because I can't manufacture what the scent of oil from an old steam engine smells like. I don't know how the corrosive odor of blackpowder and livestock mingles in the heat of the mid-day sun in a mixture potent enough to burn my nostrils.

I stare and my pace slows.

Mary tightens her grip and hauls me forward. "Keep your eyes on the horizon, Joseph. No matter how enticing this place appears, there's another storm coming."

The moment she speaks the words, the warmth slips off my shoulders and a chill wind blows against my cheeks. Instead of a crowd of happy townsfolk restocking important supplies, I now sense a shiver of despair in the hurrying pace of the crowds. People glance at the sky, their expressions saying they expect to find storm clouds gathering against the brilliant swathe of blue.

At last we reach the end of the street and duck between two buildings.

Mary gestures at a weathered building. "It's there ahead on the left. Let me enter first."

The sign nailed beside the entry reads, Portrait Maker. Before I have time to slow the pounding in my chest, and digest the possibility that Amelia is inside this ramshackle building, Mary pushes through the door and positions her body between me and the woman standing on the other side of the counter. I catch the merest glimpse of oval face and dark fabric before a male voice bellows.

"It's time you got here. Get in position."

I jump.

Turning, I find a bear in human clothing, beard bristling from the man's cheeks and plunging down his throat until his neck disappears inside the soiled collar of his oat-colored shirt.

He swings his shaggy head and glares in our direction. Small black eyes glitter from within the mass of facial hair. "Take your positions, I said. I'm losing the light already."

Mary steers me into a chair arranged before a massive canvas-covered apparatus and presses me down firm into the seat. I face the wooden interior while to my right sits the counter and front entrance. Behind me is a wall of windows designed to capture all the natural light possible. I know nothing about antique camera equipment, but I think flash powder is used to create enough illumination to expose the plate. Instead of thinking more on that, I concentrate on breathing and wondering if my increased pulse rate is a sign of impending explosion.

"Turn the boy around; I want to look at his face."

My shoulders tense but Mary increases the pressure on her palm in such a way that I understand to stay put.

"He cannot see. There is no point."

Her articulation is precise, better even than my English teacher at school.

A grumbling response is the portrait maker's singular reaction.

A slight figure slides into position beside me. I glance over using just my eyeballs to see the dark fabric and recognize the tiny flowered print worn by the person behind the counter. A delicate hand flutters down to rest on my arm and a barrage of flashes began.

Phosphorescent bursts of ignited chemical produce blinding strikes of light. Though I face away from the apparatus, my eyes still burn and water, the pungent smoky scent searing my nostrils. I fight the urge to cough.

The woman-who-might-be-Amelia digs her fingers into my bicep but makes no other movement. I think, maybe, I have gone a little mad. Mary's whisper comes near again at my ear.

ALTERNATE ENDINGS

"On the count of three."

She counts down. The last number falls from her lips and the sky goes dark with clouds. A fork of lightning splits the gloom. I am on my feet and pulling the two women alongside me, headed for the door.

I count silently one-Mississippi, two-Mississippi, three-Mississippi, four-Mississippi...we reach the doorway. And the world explodes.

I've watched the vintage footage of atomic testing in the atolls in my third period history class. I remember how the detonation funneled up and bloomed into an obscene bulbous cloud, resembling nothing so much as a poisonous toadstool.

Though my eyes are closed, the flash is blinding.

I wonder if this is how my relatives lose their eyesight. I don't pause when the roar of rage comes from behind us. I shove forward, shoulders set like I'm aiming for the opposing team's defensive line. We leap off the steps into the streets of Eternity. The fingers of each of my hands are locked around the narrow wrists of a woman. I am the link chaining my aunt and sister together.

We land on the pristine lawn of my front yard. Well, technically, it's mom and dad's house.

The fall knocks the hat off my head. I sprawl in the damp grass, disoriented and gasping for breath, shell-shocked likes a trench soldier from World War I.

A quick glance shows Aunt Mary in a graceful recline, her purple glasses askew, her eyes no longer a milky white but a brilliant turquoise blue. She winks at me and straightens the spectacles.

I roll over and come face-to-face with an older version Amelia.

She squeals and falls against me, arms wrapped tight around my throat, making happy sounds.

Bewildered and thankful though I feel, I'm glad when my dad pries Amelia loose. Mom realizes her daughter has come home and makes a sound I've never heard. I cry a little bit.

I stay on the porch after everyone else sweeps inside. Aunt Mary sits with me, rocking back and forth in a slow swing, silent as ever.

"Did we just—"

"This is who we are, Joseph." Mary's voice is soft and unequivocal.

I have no idea what she means. Her lips curl up at the edges like a satisfied kitten and I know she's amused with me again.

She looks toward me but all I can see are those dratted purple lenses. "We slip into other timelines and straighten out the chronology when it gets wrinkled. I'm going to teach you how to do it right, Joseph."

"But I'm not even finished with high school," I blurt out, failing to suppress the shiver of dread crawling through my stomach.

Aunt Mary laughs and when her mirth ends she speaks in a soft voice. "True enough. That gives us two more years to train."

7 THE BEAST WITHIN

❧

SAVANNAH WATCHED THE sparrow dart from branch to stem and experienced envy. The tiny feathered wingtips brushed against the dark burl as the bird dipped inside each white flower, systematically milking the tree of nectar. With everything that had happened in the previous six months, she most missed her freedom. In just the last week the tight buds on the tips of every bare twig had unfurled into wide leaves and the greenery clustered in thick swatches. She'd enjoyed watching the change and checked the progress of leaf-expansion each morning, something she'd never have had time to do in the past. Every day she delighted in the simple fact of being alive to welcome these hints of spring. No one remained to criticize the hours she spent contemplating natural beauty.

Even as a child, her interest in music and poetry puzzled her folks. As geneticists interested in unraveling the mystery of noncoding DNA, she was an anomaly, the offspring reflecting recessive traits her parents carried but never expressed. Her mother and father had loved her but their shared interest in the laboratory came before all else. They studied eukaryotic microbiology, their life goal intent on making the junk encoding in DNA initiate active protein sequences. The successful decoding of the human genome had been celebrated with champagne and animated discourse in their household. She remembered that evening with a sad smile; it had taken place just before her mother's terminal diagnosis.

Savannah would never forget her father's intensity the morning after her mother's funeral, him standing with one hand on the front doorknob as he studied her grim expression.

"Imagine the possibilities, Savannah." Her father said, shaking a sheaf of papers toward the general direction of the outside world, his words tumbling out in an excited rush. "We're so close to a break-through. Medical conditions like your mother's cancer might be reversed, cured, perhaps even eliminated."

Even grief for his wife failed to veil the feverish glow of fanaticism in his eyes. The lure of his scientific labors tugged him back to the emotional neutrality of the lab.

The laboratory became his domain, a kingdom which controlled his waking hours. And Savannah mourned alone. Two years later he died of an aneurism. The cleaning staff found him slumped over his desk, his work still spread out beneath his body. Savannah missed her nerdy parents every day.

It was natural that the unfinished project was bequeathed to the surviving part of the research team, Dr. Vanderskin. He paid his respects in the typical perfunctory manner after the funeral. When nothing more was forthcoming, Savannah acknowledged the slight. In her view, she should have warranted at least an update about the project which had consumed both parents and her childhood.

Her father's favorite research assistant, Robertson Miles came to visit. Despite the man's brawny appearance, suggesting he might be an athlete, he always demonstrated refined manners in her presence. His conscientious attention to propriety charmed and amused her. She'd liked him. After her father's services, he held her trembling hands, offering condolences in his deep southern drawl. His sincerity had touched her. Enjoying the comfort of his words, she responded with effusive warmth. It wasn't until much later she worried that in her loneliness she had perhaps led Robertson on a little bit.

Six months had passed since that afternoon.

Now Savannah's world had grown small. She missed having access to the wide university lawns. The fountain spray of sparkling water rising in a shimmer of repetitive arcs before the campus center was a sight she longed to see again. But it was too dangerous to venture out, even though she suspected such concerns did not apply to her. She received special treatment. Instead, she made do with a glimpse of the topmost tier of the science tower, just visible from her bedroom window if she craned her neck hard enough. The Greek Revival architecture of the university buildings complimented the surrounding Antebellum homes of the senior personnel. She'd been fortunate her parents had purchased the eclectic stone cottage at the edge of campus when her father received his faculty appointment or she'd have been homeless too. In those first weeks after becoming an orphan, she'd been so grateful no one could make her leave the family home. After the killing started she wished the nightmare would come to a swift end.

The radio squawked on occasion, a bright note to the constant soft hum of background noise. The same two arguments played over the airwaves, familiar themes she'd listened to for weeks. The NPR broadcast announcer accused the government of creating the catastrophe, implicating that efforts to produce a genetically engineered factor for population control had gone wrong. An argumentative caller disagreed and claimed the Beast was a product of modern bio-engineering; a mutant born of the greedy private sector's attempt to play God.

Savannah knew both assumptions were incorrect.

Someone had decided to test out one of their theories, with devastating and murderous results. She wasn't a scientist, but she'd been made aware by proximity to her parents. Day in and year out she'd absorbed the details of their research, comprehending their postulations regarding the latent attributes hidden away inside human genes.

The killing had started immediately. Swift and premeditated, the culprit struck with calculated intensity, plowing through law enforcement personnel. He routed the National Guard, despite the automatic weaponry. Even the army was forced to retreat, unable to deploy the big artillery without civilian casualties. Residents near the outskirts of town were

ALTERNATE ENDINGS

able to evacuate but not in the city center or the old established university quadrant. In an effort to avoid unnecessary collateral damage, officials had concentrated on a plan of containment, sealing off the perimeter of town and airlifting supplies on to the larger rooftops. After the Beast interrupted a rescue, crashing the chopper and killing everyone aboard, the radio encouraged locals to escape unaided.

Savannah figured somebody must have made it to the outside and wondered why military snipers hadn't removed the menace. For whatever reason, the creature remained active.

Once it became apparent that officials were unable to restrain the threat, she'd found herself restricted to the courtyard. There wasn't just the monster to avoid, but the increasing number of dangerous refugees searching for food. She hated the sense of imprisonment most of all. The limestone blocks of the house provided safety and a haven of sorts, so far. The enclosed yard had become a personal paradise with the winter apples yet hanging on the tree and the promise of the garden later in the summer. Still, after her prolonged incarceration she looked down at the koi pond and gravel path winding between flower beds with a jaundiced eye. The sight of the concrete bench where she spent most afternoons reading beside the bronze sundial made her feel medieval, like a character in a fairy tale. This one, she was convinced, featured a dark ending.

If that situation weren't insult enough, the steel bars of the gate which locked at the street, promised little security against the desperate. When hunger at last forced survivors to seek out those burrowed safe inside houses and businesses, she'd have minimal protection. At least she needn't worry about that right now, though her lack of self-reliance was an increasingly reckless way to survive.

Today she prayed for fruit.

She had no need to look at the clock. The sun burned hot and high overhead. The rays shining through the cranked out window acted like heated fingertips stroking the top of her head, evidence enough that it was noon and time for his midday visit. She descended the stairs to the ground floor, unlocked and pushed open the narrow plank door. After three measured breaths she crossed the garden toward the gate. The echo of a scream reverberated off the stone walls of the enclosure. Such sounds didn't make her pause, not anymore.

She halted a safe distance from the access and waited.

From the street, a bony hand wrapped around one of the sturdy cast iron stanchions and a figure sidled into view. "Let me in, Savannah."

"You know I won't do that, Dr. Vanderskin." Savannah stopped a foot short of his grasp, avoiding the long fingers when they darted between the bars to swipe at the front of her blouse.

"Your father must have more research hidden away here. He knew exactly what would happen, had predicted with total accuracy how the transcription sequences increased at a wild rate, shot right off the charts." Swiping at the trickle of perspiration beading on his forehead, the man pushed his face against the bars and rattled the gate. "He had to have known the process to halt the mutation. I want inside to search."

Savannah refused to give ground. "I've already searched everywhere, Dr. Vanderskin. Father kept none of his documentation here, our home is too small."

ALTERNATE ENDINGS

She knew it was a simple matter of time before the acceleration degraded and the subject expired or regressed. The lab tests done on Rhesus monkeys demonstrated a 98% expiration rate. Thinking of the dead primates always made Savannah sad. The results had been the primary reason her father never breached the international code of ethics in research and administered a human test subject. The one remaining member of his team had felt no such restraint. Now they all lived with the repercussions.

He hunched his shoulders, his voice dropping to a whisper. "He's coming, girl. Can't you hear?"

"Of course I can, Dr. Vanderskin."

A sequence of shrill cries increased in tempo, indicating the Beast's approach. Another group of desperate people caught outside the safety of four walls. The thought saddened her. Perhaps the shouts had come from a failed escape attempt, more victims laid at the clawed feet of molecular progress. The truth broke her heart every day. The hard work of her parents and the sacrifices of so many had resulted in the creation of a monster, not improved health for everyone.

A foolish tragedy.

The pale ascetic face jerked and drew her line of vision. The doctor's lank grey hair, no longer combed in a neat spray across his bald nape, fluttered in greasy strands along both temples. His eyes glittered in the reflected light. "You're the one the Beast wants."

Savannah studied her father's former colleague for several long seconds before responding with a nod. "Yes, and I also know the truth."

His malevolent expression lasted a fraction of a second before he darted a nervous look over one shoulder. The intensity of his gaze, the flush of fever staining his cheeks, and the dull cadaverous tone of his skin indicated ill health.

"You should return to the lab, Dr. Vanderskin. Figure out how to stop this, reverse or switch off, the active transcription process."

His gaze veered back to her, a sneer lifting one edge of his twisted mouth but the sardonic smile faltered at her calm cadence. He pointed a bony finger at her, grunted out a curse and opened his lips to speak. "You don't want to help me—"

The snort of a heavy exhalation and the scrabble of clawed appendages against a hard surface brought the man's speech to a frightened halt.

Savannah recognized the sounds of approach.

Dr. Vanderskin fled. The soft patter of his footsteps faded the moment he rounded the corner of the tight alley.

The popping of talons puncturing brick created a sharp staccato as the creature skittered into view. He dropped down from the wall of the neighboring building with a graceful leap and paused on the other side of her flimsy gate. Tight sinew corded along limbs. Smooth muscle rippled. He assumed a relaxed pose, half-standing and half-sitting in a crouch impossible for human musculature. But then, Robert was no longer hominin by definition.

Raising her gaze, Savannah met eyes that held a sense of recognition.

Saliva sheened on the single row of sharp canid teeth. His black lips shivered back in a feral display but she had learned to recognize his fierce grimace as a smile. For a moment she experienced a hard pang of regret.

ALTERNATE ENDINGS

An unwelcome disquiet flowered into awareness, an instinctual response to finding herself the focus of a predator. She coughed and the familiar connection passed.

With delicate movements, a talon maneuvered a gobbet of meat through the bars.

Savannah swallowed back the rush of fluid in her mouth and tasted bile. She identified Robertson's regular gift of sustenance wrapped in the loose scrap of fabric as raw meat. Realization registered. He provided food for her, the predator feeding his mate. The idea made her swallow hard and shut her eyes.

He was so definitely no longer human.

In a near-complete absence of sound, the Beast departed.

Savannah fluttered her lids open and eyed the remnant of cloth. A dangling button from a ripped cuff indicated the garment had once been a red jacket. Inside was a hunk of fresh striated muscle. She gathered the ragged edges together and folded the pathetic remains into a parcel. The texture of firm tissue and hard gristle branded her palms through the tattered cloth. Hands filled with the grisly offering, she surveyed the smooth grass of the courtyard with a sinking sensation. Her gaze danced across the pockmarked surfaces. Dozens of blemishes marred the expanse, the burial sites of other such offerings.

Soon she would run out of space.

8 If You Build It...

THE FIRST THING Jake Cavanaugh noted when he staggered off the public transport shuttle was the frenetic energy outside the entrance of the Highlands Hofbrauhaus. The visual added to the headache his throbbing hangover had sprouted since he'd crawled out of the back room of the deserted Honolulu Lounge just before noon and departed the Schrodinger Valley. As the number one enforcer for the Territorial Representative, he'd already warned Herman Russ against acting on any more of his harebrained ideas. The man knew Jake roughed up the locals when they got out of hand. His job came with that role. As an emissary of the local government he was charged with reducing conflict between the miners and the tourists, something that more often than not, required a full crew of knockabouts. He maintained order among the scattered lunar colonies, ignoring the joke he needed a tin star pinned to the outside of his low gravity atmospheric environmental suit.

He slowed down his approach to study the scene. The colony of jagged crags situated at the edge of the Kepler Crater swarmed with a large crowd of laborers. Beside the door stood Russ, sole proprietor of the one bar on this side of the moon. The man directed one crew as they unloaded building materials from a hovering transport skiff. A second team continued snapping together a skeletal framework of miniscule cubicles. Pristine resin girders speared the sky. Solar collection grids already functioned, their yellow and blue light sensors blinking in an alternating rhythm. Jake could see the prefabricated modular rooms were more than half-completed. He twisted his lips into a snarl and grunted. Russ might be his favorite barkeep but he knew better than to start unauthorized new construction.

This was going to get ugly as soon as he fixed this hangover.

Russ caught sight of him and picked his way between the debris littering the site. His shouted greeting, bluff and good-natured as always, was muffled by the re-breather covering his face. The extended vent hanging down in front of the man's face swung like an elephant's trunk. Jouncing over the uneven terrain, he smacked Jake on the back with a blow that almost knocked him off his feet. He wrapped one massive hand around Jake's bicep and steered him inside the establishment.

ALTERNATE ENDINGS

Jake stripped off his re-breather, planted both elbows on the bar, and cradled his aching head between his palms. Too many samples of the local lager had affected his judgement, and not for the last time. The unfortunate occurrence was a regular event on every visit he paid to the brewpub on the eastern surge of the Plato uplands.

Russ set a glass on the wood in front of him.

Jake looked at it through his bleary vision and grimaced. He pushed his belly into the old-time wooden bar, propped one boot on the chair rung and braced the other against the brass rail. Stabilized, he considered the tall narrow cylinder of fizzy green glop. He shuddered. He'd tried this same cure before and though the experience was vile, the volatile chemistry worked. As hangover remedies went, this one sobered him up quick, especially if he didn't hurl.

Something viscous swirled inside. A trail of yellow scum slid across the interior of the glass and coiled away.

Right now his need to be sober was dire enough to warrant these measures. Rumors had been bounding over the lunar landscape for weeks. He swiveled the drink, caught another glimpse of the caldera worm, and wrapped shaky fingers around the warm tumbler. Prior experience told him to slam the fetid liquid and guzzle the contents. If he ignored the buzz of carbonation that oversaturated the mucus lining of his mouth, and just swallowed the stringy occupant, he'd feel better. Instantaneous relief. Knowing that didn't make it any easier to do.

Jake closed his eyes. He counted to three before tossing down the foul concoction. Gag reflex brought part of the slurry back up and he felt the rubbery smooth body flick against his tonsils. The slick ridges slipped over the flesh of his throat. His panicked swallow washed the slushy mass past his esophagus and the non-arthropod invertebrate hit the cauldron of acid in his stomach where it exploded. Fighting the visceral rush of nausea, Jake searched his memory for the term biophysicists used to explain the effect. The distraction worked. He managed to keep the vile sludge down.

The threat of vomit passed. A ripple of heat spread through his gut and Jake sat up straighter. His vision improved. His headache waned. Bar medicine was a public damn miracle.

The whine of vacuum vapor locks sighed as the door opened and closed again, each brief exposure allowing the cacophony of construction noise to intrude. Raised voices from outside clattered above the suction of induction pipes. The susurration of the filtering system hummed, busy refining particles of nebula dust by casting them into a reservoir of oily suspension. The result was an infusion of thin misty content combined with an oxygen rich mixture.

The sound of the life-support system comforted Jake.

Lunar residents lived under constant threat of power failure and atmospheric starvation. Every off-worlder who landed here knew the statistics. Five minutes without air was enough for hypoxia to destroy the brain. Jake hunched his shoulders in an automatic attempt to shut out the barrage of images, but the memories flooded in anyways. Six months before, an unexpected radiant spike had overloaded the energy grid at the Mount Blanc colony. The resulting tragedy still haunted his sleep. The solar array banks had ruptured under the direct intensity of the column of sunlight and created a system wide failure. Three hundred and twelve people had died.

The Territorial Representative sent Jake to collect the bodies.

His team arrived at the scene prepared for horrors but the eerie visual robbed them of their hardened bravado. Per protocol, residents had strapped themselves to grounding hooks. The corpses bobbed above the surface, as though moved by a gentle breeze, the regulation eight foot lines tethering each torso to the terra Luna. The wave of humanoid figures looked like a twentieth century art display. Every off-worlder's greatest fear was imagining their body floating off into the great blackness of the universe, drifting through eternity.

Jake had retrieved the dead. One of his rules was never asking his men to complete a task he wouldn't dirty his own hands doing. He'd tried not to look at the strangled faces behind the thin polypropylene emergency masks as he shoved aside limbs contorted from seizures. Some of the bodies had been difficult to untangle. At least there had been no kids. The moon was a strictly over-eighteen population.

The destruction of the energy production plant was a catastrophe, but the loss of the brothel was far more lamented by the populace, ninety-nine percent of which was male. The recovery crew gathered among the sizzled ruins of the White House and held a moment of silence. Nothing remained except a puddle of melted synthetic compounds and the deceased sex-workers.

The sounds of construction pulled Jake from his reverie. The clanging of tools, punctuated by curses in a language not terrestrial in origin, reminded him that he had a job to do.

He blinked, realized Russ had spoken again, and raised an eyebrow in silent query.

"I said there're big doings tonight. The Highlands is getting a new business. I just need your official signature to approve the physical changes." Russ jerked a thumb towards the exterior racket and slapped a yellow paper down on the counter. "You should hang around. There'll be lovelies promenading atop the bar tonight. The sign-up list has some real beauties."

Jake interrupted the man's narrative and jabbed the air with a finger. "It's damn near impossible to get zoning approval from the Territorial Office of Lunar Development. Ever since those xenobiologists discovered low-gravity lichen growing on the plains, they've shot down every request."

Russ shoved a beer at him and displayed his gapped tooth grin.

Jake's hand closed around the cylindrical bottle in an automatic gesture. "You know I'm the official the Territorial Rep will send out here to stop whatever crazy plan you've got cooking." He slammed half the contents, choking a little on the bitter brew.

The bartender flicked his tongue through the gap where his front teeth should have been and winked at him. The gesture distracted Jake. The story of how Russ had lost his incisors twenty years before, biting out a hostile alien's throat still freaked out the locals. The celebrity of being the single survivor of that ill-fated interstellar exchange bought the old man some slack from officials, but surely not enough for this. He drained the beer and prepared to argue.

ALTERNATE ENDINGS

"Relax, Jake. I already got approval." Russ swiped the bar with a tattered blue cloth. "Your signature is just a necessary formality."

Jake skimmed the papers. His eyes widened in disbelief as he read. The Hofbrauhaus had been granted exclusivity for a new lunar brothel. "I don't care how you managed to pull this one out of your ass, you insane old goat, but you've got my vote." He scrawled his name at the bottom of each page. It was tough to ignore Russ' gloating tone, but Jake did. "When is the official grand opening?"

"I already told you. Tonight. The girls are en route from the landing station as we speak." Russ popped his lips in a smack of appreciation. "I made sure to get a redheaded devil just for you."

Jake smirked. He'd never live down that incident involving the Widow Hoskins. Nevermind the debacle had happened ten years ago and she was now remarried and earthside. "As the proprietor of this fine establishment, I hope you've considered the fact that your celebrated new employees are facing dozens of hard riding customers. The schedule shift happens tonight, and after twenty days underground, those miners will be ready for rough trade. Earthshine brings out the lunatics. You better hire on some extra muscle."

Russ fingered his missing teeth and nodded. "That's what you're here for, Jake." He shoved another piece of paper over the scarred wooden surface. "You've been reassigned for the duration. Congratulations on being made the first official lunar lawman. You're in charge of the brand-spanking-new incorporated town of Keplerville."

Jake tried to focus on the words written on the document. The stamp of the Territorial Office blazed across the page in the typical green ink. His name was typed on the line at the top. "Well hell. I guess that means I'll be settling down."

"The crew will be putting together an office for you out on Main Street, once they're done with the important stuff." Russ slid another beer down the counter toward him. "Here, Marshall. Have a freebie on the house."

9 LATE FOR LIFE

KNUCK RESTED A CALLOUSED palm against the damp bricks of the abandoned pharmacy and coughed until his chest burned. One of these days the fit wasn't going to pass until he keeled over dead. He stabilized his posture, planted his feet wide and with precise aim, spat the blood-tinged sputum in the gutter. He slapped at the surface of the weathered brick with an affectionate palm, swept away by nostalgia.

October always marked the return of the rainy season and brought to mind his first job in the wharf district. He'd been an unskilled lob-lolly, humping crates of imported goods from the dock loaders up to this building in the pouring rain.

Thirty-five years ago, he'd been a bulky fourteen-year-old capable of out-lifting men twice his age. Desperate to prove himself, the port bosses worked him till he dropped. The strength training he'd gotten on the job translated to his success in the sparring ring and he'd climbed the boxing ranks fast. In his prime, Knuck could go a hundred rounds without fatigue, taking hits capable of felling other men.

Now it felt like someone else's history.

The true irony was he'd outlived everybody. Old industries had given way to mechanized methods. Today's commerce involved more production and less labor. This new world valued machines over people. The businesses that had built the city into a trade center sat derelict, their doors and windows nailed shut. The port that once established Bricktown on maritime maps languished empty and abandoned. Even the hierarchy that ruled the neighborhoods, making them safe places for women to visit the corner market and children to play kick-the-can in the streets, had fallen to the anarchy. A steep rise in unemployment and increased lawlessness turned his thriving community into a ghost town. Worse yet, he was the only one left to voice questions about the night Rosie disappeared. Any mention of her name or thought associated with then, was enough to send him spiraling back through the litany of details burned into his memory. Her loss became the measure of time by which all things were judged in his life.

Gin had dulled his guilt over the years, but regrets too numerous to acknowledge had stacked up around him like cordage forming an invisible funeral pyre. A single stray spark could consume the fractured ruin of his existence, a bonfire of minimal proportions compared to what his person-

ALTERNATE ENDINGS

al history might have been. Rosie went missing and everything had gone to hell. The biggest change of late was how the waterfront matched Knuck's internal landscape.

He pushed off the wall and tapped another cigarette out of the crumpled box. He never slowed his pace as he lit the tip. Even now, lungs half-eaten by consumption, he took down men half his age. The tattooed bastards roaming the district today didn't know how to shrug off a punch or throw one. *Punks*. He sucked in deep, enjoyed the flash of pain in his lungs, fought a spasm and managed to fend off another coughing attack. The hot vapors of smoke no longer fed the intense ache inside him. The sorrow had become a kernel of misery, something hardened and fossilized by the passage of years.

He swiveled to position his good ear and listened.

The crisp footfalls increased in tempo.

Here came another joker determined to learn the hard way that Knuck wasn't an easy mark. Twenty-feet farther down the sidewalk, he flicked the unfiltered cigarette stub out on the wet pavement, watching the nub tumble and bounce twice before the tiny red coal winked out. Veering down a narrow alley, Knuck flexed his fingers and twisted his elbows, limbering his stiff joints. A couple of quick body jabs and the bozo following him would go down hard. Knuck planned to step over the bastard's sprawled form and be on his way again, headed home to an empty room and his solitary life.

Bricktown was absent of nightlife, even though it was an hour shy of midnight on a Friday. No one came here anymore. The old entertainments were long gone. Not like in the glory days when the waterfront was a raucous bedlam of unsavory entertainment, a place of enticing and alluring danger, attracting rich and poor alike. Regular police sweeps had purged the destitute and itinerant from public view as the mayor's revitalization plan for the decrepit port district gained favor. Knuck hated the thought of even more change. He knew these streets. The narrow labyrinthine channels cutting between the custom houses and charging sheds were familiar trails.

He cut down an alley, stopped again to turn his head and listen, his mouth twisting into a smirk. His pursuer had faltered at the entrance to the dark lane. To the uninitiated, the cramped shadowed alley should cause even an unwary man a moment of hesitation. Satisfaction surged inside him when the steps resumed. At least this bastard had big enough balls to follow him into the labyrinth. Pummeling his fists into an adversary brought Knuck a small measure of release, a way to expel the anger and torment buried deep in his psyche. He wanted that tonight.

Knuck waited. He counted the man's steps, holding himself silent near the wall of a building, still as a statue in the gloom. His quarry arrived, stepping into view. Knuck lunged out of the shadows. The challenge he'd prepared to issue clotted in his throat at the sight of the gun in the other man's hand.

Seconds elapsed.

A barrage of disjointed thoughts and visceral memories jounced through Knuck's mind in random trajectories. Eyes fixated on the bizarre firearm, he tried to make sense of what he was seeing. Never had he viewed such a pistol. Brass gleamed on the dials sticking out above the grip. Copper diodes were stacked in a row down one side of the barrel. Blue light arced across a gap to strike the cathode amidst searing snapping pops, and repeated. The device looked like one of the gadgets featured on the Nikola Tesla exhibit posters that were splashed over all the midtown trolley cars. The gauge of the tri-power cylinder was massive, larger than the .45 tucked inside the baggy pants of the punk who'd attempted to rob Knuck last Monday.

A cinematic quality defined the appearance of the man holding him at gunpoint. A charcoal colored trench coat concealed most of a muscular build, but it was the man's calm demeanor that fascinated Knuck. Chilled mercury slid through this guy's veins. The black Homburg and upturned collar obscured the gunman's features, but Knuck's attention focused on the broad square jaw which rivaled his own before scanning down. The stranger's fancy grey-striped trousers were pleated in the front, similar in style to the ones worn in old formal photographs. Immaculate hard-soled leather shoes rang clear in the silence under the steel trestles of the St. John's Bridge.

The weapon jerked to the left. "Let's get moving. We're on the clock."

Knuck hesitated, weighed his options, and then obeyed with sloth-like movements.

The man waved him toward one of the hulking cement abutments that made up the stanchions of the bridge. "You've been a difficult guy to locate. Now it's time to clear the books and start over." His fingers clenched around the gun's handgrip.

The piece looked heavy to Knuck. Fluorescence flashed along the muzzle and the sound of electricity crackled in response. He squinted into the glow and though he failed to recognize the man's indistinct features, he was struck anew by a puzzling familiarity. Certain he'd never tangled with this fellow because he'd remember the big sonovabitch, no matter how much gin he'd drank to deaden the past, he decided to pass.

"You got the wrong guy, mister." Knuck said.

"Do you think so?" The stranger mocked.

Frustrated by the sudden need to piss, Knuck shifted his weight and attempted to ignore the protests of his strained bladder. Multiple kidney hits had worsened the effect of too many years of hard living. In his battered body, a steady stream sometimes felt more satisfying than sex. It might be worth getting shot with the weird gun just to finish this business so he could take a leak. He made another attempt. "Let's shake and call this an honest mistake."

An amused baritone chuckle rolled from beneath the hat; white teeth glinted between lips curved in a lopsided grin. "But aren't you Calvin-no-middle-name-Manchester, the youngest son of Robert and Beatrice, and former bareknuckle boxing champion of the North Side?"

Knuck went still. Every nerve in his body sang with alertness. *What the hell?* Nobody knew the names of his parents. Christ, there was no one left alive who remembered his given name.

Adrenalin rocketed through his circulatory system in a hissing rush, his chest muscles tensed as if for the ringside bell to clang. Knuck inhaled a sharp breath. Reluctant, he nodded. "That's me."

The man in the hat pointed up at the sky with his unencumbered hand and twirled a finger indicating the area. "Don't you recognize this place?"

ALTERNATE ENDINGS

Knuck raised his gaze to span the art deco architecture. The graceful lines of the elegant arches sat silhouetted against the fathomless gloom of the dark sky. He knew the bridge, all right. Not far from here was the fateful place he should have met his wife so many years before. He recalled every detail of that night with startling clarity. Afterwards his world went numb. Everything good had been stripped from his life.

All because he'd been late.

"I know it," he ground the words out through clenched teeth.

The man moved his index finger and the weapon came alive. A pearlescent drop of glowing viscous plasma streamed like molten honey from the end of the spinning barrel. A burst of light illuminated the scene. Atmospheric discharge haloed the two men in a sparking voltaic glow. He got a clear look at the face of his captor, and the weight of recognition seeped through Knuck.

Time stretched out, drew thin.

The mist turned into a fine rain. The normal sounds of night receded, became auditory illusions. A car horn blared and faded. Glass shattered and echoed. The slap of water splashing up the pilings intensified. A distant rumble came from underground. The sound preceded an explosion of steam, advancing in a predatory line by virtue of subterranean channels. Plumes of vapor erupted at measured intervals from the street grates.

The stranger tilted up the brim of his hat and displayed a face that was unfamiliar and yet not unknown. "I confess the stories don't do you justice. I thought most of them must be exaggerations." Motioning again with the strange firearm, he indicated the direction they should move.

Knuck shook off a momentary confusion. His assailant's words made no sense but the younger man grinned at him as if they were familiar acquaintances. Curiosity overrode his anger. The odd familiarity gnawed at him. Had he known the kid's father? Maybe the gun was revenge for an old wrong. Knuck had been guilty of picking enough fights, especially after Rosie disappeared.

They skirted the gigantic foundation of the main escutcheon until they reached a portal. Knuck stopped and stared. The door was mounted to the structural support like a submarine hatch. Iron rivets the size of a man's fist affixed the thick metal plate to the concrete column. He'd passed this way a thousand times and never seen it before. He pointed at the access panel. "What the hell's that?"

Appreciative mirth spilled out of the stranger's mouth. "I was told you'd balk at every order and question everything." The stranger winked at him. "The clock is ticking, time is running down. Just turn the crank and open the past. Your future is damned tired of waiting."

Heart knocking against his ribs, Knuck swung around to peer at the intricate brass inlay decorating the edge of the portal. His gaze locked on the copper-clad hand wheel. Hope sang through him, obscene in its intensity. He tried not to speak but the question fumbled out. "Who's on the other side?"

"Your wife."

The words hit Knuck like hammer blows. His knees went weak at the possibility. Nothing else mattered. He stumbled forward, the stranger forgotten, his scarred fingers wrapping over the cold bronze of the crank. He spun the oiled bearings, heaved on the heavy panel, and yanked the steel hatch wide. He heard the gun discharge. A blistering solar flare of illumination engulfed his body from behind. In the harsh light, Knuck watched the blood vessels, a veil of indigo webs crossing the back of his hands, firm into youthful resilient skin. Blinded, he fell in, landing amid a welcoming cocoon of arms. He recognized her scent in an instant.

"Rosie. I found you." He whispered. "I must be dead."

A smooth cheek rubbed along his, warm lips pressed his temple, and then long fingers pinched his bicep. Hard. "Don't be an ass, Knuck. I sent Junior to find you."

10 Crossing the Water

ZEKE HADN'T EXPERIENCED a single visitation in the week since he'd burned down the house. Seven nights of uninterrupted sleep had been bliss, adjusting to life in the garage, not so much. The wooden structure leaned to one side like a drunken hobo, the rafters bowed from eighty years of deferred maintenance. The interior looked more like the skeletal ribcage of a leviathan nightmare creature than a place to set up housekeeping. He'd stacked the cans of decades-old solvents beside the half-empty paint containers and laid boards across the lids to create shelves for his meager belongings. Even with the concrete slab foundation, the dilapidated place was still in better condition than the house had been, it being fifty years older yet.

He shivered from the damp cold. Sputters of near-boiling water accompanied the drip of brown liquid through the filter and produced a fragrant steam. Taste buds flickering, Zeke's mouth watered. He bent his head over the battered Mr. Coffee he'd bought from the second-hand store to inhale the moist flavor. This early in the morning he found the smell of fresh-ground beans as stimulating as the scent of sexy female late at night.

He scratched at the waistband of his sweats, the garment hanging off his lean hips. The chill rising up from the floor shriveled his nutsack tight as a walnut.

Swapping the carafe for a mug, he filled the cup two-thirds full with the extra strong brew. Impatient, he burned his tongue trying to suck in caffeine. The shelter offered meager protection from Georgia's wet March wind, so he shuffled back to his makeshift bed in the corner. He hadn't asphyxiated himself with the propane heater. That was a plus. Things were looking up.

Score two for Zeke-the-Arsonist.

The rest of Rawlton's inhabitants thought he was a tub-thumping lunatic. He didn't blame the townsfolk since all the old-timers knew the family line *wasn't* quite right. Hell, twelve generations back, the Holsbrooks had proved they were batshit loony when they settled the bottomlands of Jasper County.

He rummaged around with one foot until he rooted out his last pair of clean socks, bending over to tug them on one at a time, the hot cup cradled in one hand. Laundry would be quick now that he only owned three sets of clothes. He balanced the mug on the bumper of his truck, yanking jeans on over his sweats. He stuffed his feet inside sneakers and pulled a sweatshirt over his head. As he pushed out the faded crewneck binding, he focused on the wrinkled face of the old man just inches away. A yelp squeezed out of his mouth.

Zeke fell back on the mound of clothes on his bed. "Holy shit, Gramps. You scared the hell out of me." He peered closer. His heart thudded. "Ah fuck..." The telltale grey glow burned in his grandfather's eyes. "Firing up the house was supposed to break the cycle."

His grandfather shrugged. "Didn't work. Get off the floor, you look like an idiot."

Zeke climbed to his feet. He watched Gramps turn and shuffle toward the folding chairs, sitting down as if he still had a corporeal body. When had the old man died? Yesterday morning he'd cut through the woods, balancing on the slick moss-covered surface of the downed log that served as a bridge over the creek, to help Gramps stack a load of firewood inside his little house. The stream, already swelled with rainwater from the winter downpour, had reached a dangerous high mark when he crossed back over at lunchtime.

"Anyone find your body yet?"

Gramps beetled his brows, then shook his head. "Don't think they will. Rained a frog-choker last night. I fell off the log into the water. Got swept clean away." His grin became a gap-toothed smile. "Too much rye," he cackled, "I'm fish food now, boyo."

Zeke retrieved the ceramic cup with the Savannah State University logo, his almost alma mater, and gulped the remaining too-hot liquid. He burned the inside of his mouth. Refilling his coffee, he added a double shot from the half-empty fifth of bourbon he'd opened two nights ago. Blowing at the oil-slicked surface, he leaned against the washing machine and inhaled alcohol vapors, contemplating his grandfather.

"Have you seen anyone?"

"You mean relatives?" Gramps crossed his right leg over his left and tilted sideways in the chair. "Nope. The family haunts all went up in smoke with the house. Must be something to that old wives' tale about fire destroying the links the dead have to life. That was good thinking, Zeke."

Zeke could see his grandfather's gaze grow distracted. The freshly deceased didn't linger long before snapping out for a siesta. He figured the transition took a while to adjust. He sipped at the alcohol-infused coffee and welcomed the jolt of heat running through his veins.

"What do you want me to do, Gramps?"

"Best call the Sheriff. Don't forget to grab the wad of cash in the inside pocket of my suit coat. You're the last Holsbrook. You spend it." He glanced around the garage. "Hell Zeke, move out of this dump. My perfectly good cabin is just beyond the hickory grove. Probably not be a bad idea to get some distance from the old homestead anyway, in case the family ghosts start resurrecting."

Gramps stared up at the trusses overhead, like he could see the morning overcast sky through the roof. He frowned as if unhappy from the lack of sunlight.

Zeke knew his grandfather had maybe a minute or two before he blinked out. "I'm sorry you went the way you did, Gramps."

The old man swiveled his head. He looked at him for a moment with no recognition and then the familiar personality slid home. He snickered. "Don't make much difference in our case, do it?"

Zeke's mouth curved into a smile. One spirit jawing in his ear was better than the hundreds buzzing around him before the fire. The number of voices whispering in his ears had driven him half-mad.

"One thing you got to know, Zeke." His grandfather's tone turned urgent. "Don't let the Sheriff poke around the woodshed. I buried the body there." The old man's attention returned to the sagging roof.

Zeke moved his lips. He opened his mouth but his vocal cords produced no sound. He exhaled and finally the words tumbled out in a breathless rush. "Who the fuck is buried out back?"

His grandfather didn't blink. "He showed up late last night, wanting to make trouble. Things just got out of hand." He lifted a lazy finger to point in Zeke's direction. "He'll be waiting for you. Sorry about that."

Darting forward, Zeke slopped coffee all over the lid of the dryer. Dread shivered through him, raised chill bumps down his arms. Murder victims were angry and violent, hard to control. "Who'd you put down, Gramps?"

His grandfather's voice was slow, his words sluggish and heavy. "An unexpected guest."

Then he blinked out of sight.

The oppressive heat of summer hung in the afternoon. Cicadas buzzed. The scent of moist soil lingered from the garden where the tomatoes and chick peas were in full flower. The live oaks surrounding the clearing dripped with bearded moss and fresh green leaves. The chill of winter was a fond memory to Zeke as he rolled the sweating beer between his palms. Four months had passed since his grandfather went missing. Officially, his presumed demise had been listed as death-by-drowning. An empty booze bottle been recovered near the stream, found with his hat, beside the felled log they'd used for a bridge.

In the interest of self-preservation, Zeke had delayed having friends over to visit after he moved in to his grandfather's small cabin in the woods. He'd been nervous somebody might figure out there was a body buried out back, but the concern had proved unfounded.

A Fourth of July BBQ offered an opportunity to round up the old gang from high school. After graduation, he'd moved off to the city and lost track of everyone. The freedom didn't last. In the second year he flunked out of college. He returned home, the cacophony of voices a constant clutter in his head. The noise worsened as he got older. The dead accumulated. The louder the chatter became, the less he could function.

He learned not much had changed with his old friends. The greedy bastards ate everything in sight, consumed all his alcohol, and departed in record time. He'd discovered one lone soldier of Cadwallader Hard Cider stripped of its sodden label. He dove on the bottle, sequestered beneath a patriotic streamer in the ice chest, popping the cap with a chortle. He tipped back the amber glass and swirled the cold tart flavor over his tongue with satisfaction.

He winced, tenderly fingering his temple where stiff stubble bristled over one eye. Hours before, a column of flame had flared up from the grill, singing his left eyebrow to the roots. The event had produced an appreciative smattering of applause from his half-drunk guests. Hoots and whistles had accompanied his frantic attempt to splash a bottle of Sweetwater brew on his forehead. The burn still stung like hell, but at least the skin hadn't blistered. He poked among the coals until he found the last foil-wrapped packed of meat. The pork shoulder fell apart in a succulent pile, the sweet vinegar brine soaking the flesh in southern-flavored perfection.

After he finished eating, Zeke debated joining the crowded fireworks display in town but decided he was too tipsy for crossing the water. The stream had already taken Gramps. Instead, he stuffed another hunk of barbecue in his mouth and went back to rooting for a beer.

Gramps manifested.

After four months of death, he was still pleased Zeke had burned their dilapidated homestead to the ground, severing the umbilical cord connecting their collective ancestry to this world. The afterlife was quieter as a result, as was Zeke's life.

"How's it hanging?" Zeke asked.

"I know you were raised better, but to the right like always." His grandfather dropped on to a lawn chair. "Your grandmother was a church-going woman. She kept me accountable to a mighty narrow line. Seeing as how I slipped off the path once or twice, I'm relieved to elude an eternity with her harping on my indiscretions."

Zeke tried to ignore this admission of marital infidelity. He'd loved his grandmother but her constant litany of scolds was one of the primary reasons he'd set the house afire.

A second man winked into view. This new companion was the victim buried under the woodshed, a situation Zeke had yet to reconcile. The fact Joe Morovsky had been both a cousin and a cop complicated the issue. Since he was family, Zeke now had him forever, unless he burned down Gramps' place. Which would leave him back in the garage. No go, there.

Joe floated forward. He eyed the remnants of barbecued pork on the paper plate. "I miss food."

Zeke dismissed the mournful note in the man's tone. "For being such a badass you were stupid enough to get whacked by an old codger."

Joe flipped him a lazy bird. "In truth, I wasn't that good of a cop." He angled his head as if listening to something. "A Sheriff's deputy is parking his car over by the former Holsbrook family homestead." His gaze lurched to Zeke's and he arched his eyebrows. "I keep telling you it's a risky proposition, leaving my corpse buried out back."

Gramps nodded his agreement. "I've come round to his way of thinking, boyo. You should move the remains."

Zeke pinched the bridge of his nose. He refused to dig up Joe's stinking body. "Maybe when there's nothing but bones left." And not even then.

"If a cadaver dog gets one whiff of my carcass, you'll be riding the big bus." Joe grinned. "Well possibly not, since you weren't the bastard who hit me with a shovel, but you should call the Sheriff anyway. Tell him something stinks powerful bad. He'll blame the old coot." He pointed a finger at Gramps.

His grandfather sat up straighter, intrigued by the idea. "Town's hankering for new gossip. People done speculated themselves out deciding why you burnt up the house." He rotated toward the stream. "Deputy Collier's coming across the creek. He's carrying something official."

ALTERNATE ENDINGS

A minute later the officer pushed aside the dangling branches of the broadleaved magnolia. He called out a greeting. "Hey, Zeke. I got some paperwork with your name on it." He lifted his hand to show him an envelope. "This came down from the state office." His voice deepened as he pressed forward to dispatch the delivery. "It's been on the duty desk all week. I thought I'd do the official serving."

Zeke drained the remaining cider, reaching over to accept the envelope. "Am I in trouble?" He gone to high school with the deputy but Collier had been two grades ahead. Now he couldn't remember the guy's given name. The deputy was one of those guys surrounded by positive stuff, everything in his life working out for the better. Blessed with his dad's handsome genes, a strong physique, and enough brains to land a good job in law enforcement—the man had even married the homecoming queen. A fiver said he owned a golden retriever, had produced the regulation 2.4 kids, and lived in a house circled by a white picket fence.

Zeke feel like a complete loser.

The deputy shook his head. "Of course not, Zeke. I know you've had a tough year, what with the fire and then your granddad's accident. Just read the letter inside, okay?" The man compressed his lips tight together and stuck out his hand. "I always thought you were a decent guy who got some raw breaks. I'm real sorry about your grandfather."

Zeke was surprised by the gesture. Guys like Collier never made time for misfits. He fumbled with the envelope, tucking the cider bottle under one arm to free up a hand to exchange a limp shake.

"Thanks, I appreciate that." And he did. It was nice someone had noticed he wasn't an actual head-case, even if Collier didn't know the real circumstances.

After the deputy was swallowed up by the woods, Zeke frowned down at the printed return address of a social services agency. He tore open one end of the envelope and tapped loose a single sheet of paper. Unfolding the document, he ignored the curious looks from his grandfather and cousin. As he scanned the text, the happy booze buzz in his head burgeoned into a clanging security alarm. Eyes widening, his breaths shallowed out as the content of the letter digested.

"Holy hell." His whisper contained a hint of panic.

"Zeke?" Gramps rose to his feet, a note of concern in his expression. He passed through the still-smoking barbecue pit as he approached.

Zeke tossed the empty Cadwallader bottle in the recycle bucket. The glass landed with a resounding crash as he turned and glared at Joe.

"You're a complete dumbshit."

Joe appeared affronted.

Gramps wore his puzzled expression, the skin between his eyes winkled into a series of folds and his mouth a slight bit open.

Zeke rattled the letter for emphasis. "This writ notifies me you were killed in the line of duty while employed by the State Office of Criminal Investigation. *Two months ago.*" Zeke speared his grandfather with a glance. "We all know that's not what happened."

"Could be it's a mistake." Gramps darted a look at Joe.

Zeke looked at his cousin but Joe's features had gone blank. He prodded him by thrusting the letter at his nose.

ALTERNATE ENDINGS

"That's not likely." Joe said. "The technology today makes it difficult to misidentify a body —"

Zeke waved them silent. "Oh, but wait, there's more." Huffing with indignation, he reviewed the passage. "You're dead. The government has identified me as your immediate next-of-kin. I inherit everything."

Gramps elbowed Joe in the ribs. "Leave the boy anything good?"

Joe scowled. "Now there's some fucked up irony. Don't count on shit from me, Zeke. I was a public servant. My car was leased. The apartment I rented was filled with cheap IKEA furniture. My bank balance hovered at zero by the end of every pay cycle."

Fury flushed Zeke's pale cheeks. "Can't think of anything else, eh? That says a lot, asshole." He swiveled to meet Gramp's eyes. "The final paragraph requires me to appear before the State Judicial Court on July 25th. I've been declared the legal guardian of five-year-old Lilliana Buchanan Morovsky." He jabbed the air in front of Joe's nose. "*Your daughter.*"

The other man's face took on a shocked expression. He lost his grip on the corporeal world and blinked out.

Gramps sidled closer. "Well, I'll be jimmied."

Zeke ignored the muttered words. He re-read the letter. No matter how many times he searched the sentences for an alternate meaning, the results were the same.

He looked at his grandfather. "There has to be some mistake. I can't be the only person left alive who is related to this little girl."

Gramps shrugged. "You're the last Holsbrook left around these parts, Zeke."

Joe rematerialized without warning. He crowded in, peering across Zeke's collar, to read over his shoulder. When he spoke his voice had gone flat, containing no hint of his normal inflection. "Angela Buchanan never told me we had a child."

Personally, Zeke thought that reflected on the sort of guy she thought Joe had been. Not daddy material.

"I heard that Angela died in a car accident last November, but I didn't go to the funeral." He looked guilty. "I was working on a case and had heard she was going to get married next summer. I didn't want to be intrusive."

A silence filled the room.

"Happy Independence Day, Zeke," Gramps cackled with mirth. "Congratulations. You're a family man now."

Zeke swayed. "I need another drink."

Zeke scratched his ear. He ignored the shape of his grandfather sitting in the chair by the window. The old guy looked good. There were days that he thought death had improved the old guy's overall health. Hiking the blanket over his head, he rolled over and tried to drown out the words. His grandfather's measured tones permeated the cotton barrier.

"You gotta step up and do this thing, boyo. It's only right that Lilliana be with family."

Zeke frowned. The covers failed to muffle his sarcasm. "You really think I'm the relative she needs for a homeroom mother?"

His grandfather made a so-so noise.

Zeke threw back the bedcovers. He glared toward the window. The fierceness of his scowl, bolstered by his bleary eyes and three days of beard growth, failed to impress his grandfather. "Joe didn't even know his daughter existed until I read the letter from the state." He scanned the room. "Where the hell is he? Every morning he's in here griping as soon as the sun rises."

Gramps shrugged, his normal response to any question he had no interest in answering. "Regardless of the circumstances, this is the way of things now."

Zeke ignored the sympathy on the old man's face. He shoved his fingers through his hair and yawned, returning to his earlier theme. "Notice that I don't mention how you're the one responsible for my current predicament, seeing as how you offed Joe. Then you went and drowned yourself in the creek."

Gramps grinned. "I told you that was an accident. Both times. I'd never have hit him with the shovel if he hadn't popped around the corner of the house. He startled me. What cop does that? Damn near gave me heart palpitations. Afterward, I had me a little too much rye juice, trying to feel better with the whole business. I drank most of the bottle just so I could get through the burying process. Then I slipped off that damned log. You should build a bridge, Zeke."

"Don't change the subject, Gramps. You know I'm not fit to raise a kid, in particular a girl one."

His grandfather laughed at him.

"I'm a worthless, lazy spendthrift, and a drunk. You've said so yourself."

"Hell, Son. That just makes you a dyed-in-the-pants Holsbrook. Besides, it's my job to motivate you to do better."

Zeke sent him a speaking look.

"C'mon now. You told the court you'd take in that little girl. Now, you've had a nice bender, but this is the time to get yourself cleaned up and stop sucking hind titty." Gramps said in a stern voice.

Zeke collapsed back on the bed. "Where's Joe?"

"He's trying to figure out who faked his death after he died."

Zeke thought this news for a moment. That detail worried him too. If somebody wanted Joe Morovsky dead for a reason, the matter seemed destined to somehow land on his doorstep.

"Do you think I should tell Deputy Collier there's somebody buried under the woodpile? I could make up some reason to dig around and find his corpse. The identification of a second Joe Morovsky might stir things up."

Gramps screwed up his lips. He hesitated before responding. "I think you should hold off. Someone already whacked a stick against the proverbial beehive. I'm unsettled by Joe being declared dead and you inheriting his daughter."

Zeke sat up, his gaze sharpening. This was too close to his concerns. "What is it Gramps? You sense something?"

He nodded. "Get ready, son. There's load of fuck-all coming down the road. Lilliana is in danger. We're all the people she's got left."

That was catalyst enough. Zeke climbed out of bed and pulled himself together.

11 THE UNEXPECTED END

P AUL FEARED EVERYONE he'd ever known was dead. Every single person on the planet might even be gone. He might be the last human left alive. Standing in the doorway of his apartment trying not to hyperventilate, he wasn't sure how he felt about that idea. His father, a minister of the blackest cloth but also a realist in regard to his son's future prospects, would've claimed that fact as evidence of God's sense of humor. The survivors of any apocalypse had to be surprised to find themselves the last ones standing. Even Paul could recognize irony when it hit like a sledge hammer.

His roommate Jorge lay sprawled on the couch in front of the flat screen. A rerun of SpongeBob SquarePants blared from the television. The box of Captain Crunch had upended, scattering sugared pillows across the pebbled texture of the beige upholstery. A minute earlier he'd stumbled over the visual. Spurred into a panicked retreat but unable to tear his gaze from the scene, he backed out of the apartment, tripped over the body of an elderly neighbor and fell. He shoved against the filthy carpet of the hallway, digging the heels of his work boots into the frayed surface in a frantic attempt to avoid touching the corpse.

Mrs. Stemler's appearance brought a fresh wave of nausea. Her face was a tiny wrinkled heap above the gaping neckline of her threadbare housecoat. The old woman's huge eyes were wet-looking, magnified behind thick prescription lenses. A lump of what might have been Raisin Bran stained her dentures. The clawed grip of her gnarled right hand held a half-crushed Coors Light can.

An instinctive flight response kicked in. Adrenalin flowed. Paul fled.

At the end of the hall, he found the coeds who lived in 11B. Dressed in form-fitting workout clothes, they lay in a neat row at the top of the stairs where they'd collapsed. Their yoga mats piled up near the threshold reminded him of brightly-colored monstrous Tootsie rolls. His leap over the threesome would have impressed an Olympic judge, except he landed on a half-eaten energy bar and skidded for a foot-and-a-half before crashing face-first into the steel fire door. Knocked half-unconscious, he pushed off the frame, overcorrecting his balance until he found his footing. He accidently kicked the shoulder of the brunette he'd always thought the prettiest, and burst out with an apology. "Sorry! Sorry!"

ALTERNATE ENDINGS

He scrambled down the staircase, one palm clasped to his forehead, escaping into the bright sunlight. Averting his face from the ground-floor unit where the single mom lived required deliberate effort. Just thinking of her tow-headed kids heaved scorching bile up his esophagus.

Chest thumping and stomach churning, he bolted down the street.

The silence of the empty town chilled him, the unnatural stillness pushing him farther. Paul ran harder. Legs pistoning, arms pumping, he continued until his anatomy quivered. Chest threatening to seize, he stumbled as the panic receded. He found himself standing on an expansive green lawn. The buildings were recognizable as his old high school. He staggered but kept his balance while he gulped air into his strained lungs. At least no bodies littered the scene here. If he shut out the events of the previous fifteen minutes, he could almost believe none of the horror had happened. Warm sun soothed his face as his muscles relaxed. The sweet smell of cut grass lulled him into a semblance of calm.

Think. Just think.

Thank god class sessions didn't run this late in the summer. Dozens of lifeless teens dropped dead, lolling boneless and androgynous as video game characters, would have turned him into a spineless wreck. Frantic to shut down the images filling his mind, he suppressed a shudder and spun in a circle. Right now he needed to maintain his fragile composure.

A figure barreled around the corner of the science complex.

Paul straightened. He whooped out a sound to attract attention.

The newcomer altered his trajectory, sprinting toward him.

He instantly recognized Ethan, his best friend from childhood. A kernel of data popped in Paul's mind, connecting to the fact both of them had survived, but he had no time to study the notion before Ethan rammed into him. Grabbed in a one-armed hug, Paul slapped his old friend's shoulder. Impossible as it seemed, graduation had been four years ago, but after this morning it was another lifetime altogether. They knocked fists in the middle of the manicured green where they'd once played football, snuck cigarettes and lied about snagging girls.

Ethan leaned down, gasping for air, his pale cheeks sucking in with each strident breath. His animated features were slack with shock.

"Thank god you came here," Paul said, a relieved grin stretching his mouth.

"Dude! Lewis face-planted in his Cheerios, right at the kitchen table." He jerked a cigarette pack loose from his pocket, shaking out a filtered Marlboro. His hands trembled so hard it took three tries to light the tip. He sucked deep. Smoke expelled in a stuttered stream, along with his words. "At first I thought he was hung over." He shrugged, jerking his head twice to the left. "You know, like usual." He exhaled again, his voice growing ragged as the words poured out. "I found Mike in his room, collapsed next to his Xbox with *Fable III* still playing on the screen. Fritos all over the floor. Even his fucking cat was dead."

"Jeezus, that sucks." Paul guy-punched Ethan in the shoulder, hard enough to push them both sideways, knocking them both off-balance.

ALTERNATE ENDINGS

Hunched over low, Ethan worked at catching his breath, puffing out more clouds of smoke in between gasps.

Coughing hoarsely into his shirtsleeve, Paul gaze roved the landscape. "Remember, when we were growing up, my dad preached at us during every dinner? He nailed the end times into our psyches. Told us to get ready. It was always 'prepare for the Lord's deliverance and pass the lima beans' or some shit."

Ethan mopped his forehead with the tail of his dress shirt. "I remember. Your dad was ready to rumble when it came to religion."

Swiping the pack of smokes, Paul lit one for himself.

Ethan dropped the burning butt, ground the filter into the soft turf beneath his sneaker, and reached out his fingers, grasping for another.

"You know what?" Paul handed back the crumpled package. He struck a match to light both tips. "I'm relieved he died earlier this year. This would have pissed him off. Can you imagine preparing your whole life for the last bang, only to choke off when it happened? Brutal man."

"I'll give that an amen." Ethan craned his head, stretching his neck to look in all directions. "I imagined at least zombies."

"No shit!"

They finished smoking and made a decision. Traversing the empty field, they loped down an alley to the main thoroughfare. After peering past the granite blocks forming the Second Mercantile Bank, they sprinted across to the local brewpub, ignoring the grotesque arrangement of bodies inside every automobile.

"If we survived, there must be others. How many do you think are left?" Ethan pushed open the unlocked door. He scanned the interior. Stepping over a workman's dolly still holding half a dozen cases of lager, he walked toward the bar. He lurched around the end, yanked the walk-in cooler access wide and plunged inside.

Paul hawked. He spat in one of the empty cartons tumbled on the floor beside a barstool. "You know the statistics as well as I do, somewhere near ten-to-fifteen percent of the population." He started at the pair of denim-clad legs protruding from behind a wall of boxes. "Hey man, we need a plan. July's a bad month to be in a burg whose inhabitants are ready to push up daisies. Think about how many folks are above ground."

Ethan reappeared, his arms filled with beverages.

Paul caught the Aquafina bottle on reflex. He twisted off the lid, guzzling the contents in a flash, throwing the drained empty over his shoulder. He approached the bar, taking a second one from Ethan's outstretched hand.

"I've got an awesome idea. We could head for my uncle's cabin at Lancaster Lake. It's remote. We might have to plant a few bodies." Ethan winked. "My Dad's bat-shit crazy brother lives out there. He hunts all his own food. He's like us, which means he should still be kicking."

Paul raised his Aquafina in a toast. "Let's grab an SUV, ransack some stores, and blow this graveyard."

Ethan clashed his plastic bottle against Paul's. "I never thought I'd say this, but thank god for gluten allergies."

12 Like Shadow in Moonlight

CORPORAL EVANS PARKED his military issued vehicle. He took a single deep breath, swallowing his nervousness as he climbed out of the driver's side door, careful to keep his stiff posture. His head still spun from the sudden avalanche of events that had taken place this evening. He shouldered his gear and crossed the road to meet his contact. Stopping in front of the man, he came to attention, offered a crisp salute and reported as he'd been directed.

The man in the black fatigues seized his hand in a firm grip and gave a vigorous shake. "Welcome to the game, Corporal. My name is Dutch. You've been assigned to this team because your psych tests demonstrate the right set of abilities."

Evans worked to keep his expression neutral. He had no idea what special skills the army thought he owned.

Dutch continued to speak even though he was giving him the once over. "On this assignment we function as a cohort, therefore, we operate as equals. Make no mistake, Corporal, I'm the one in charge but you need to speak your mind at all times. Don't hesitate to offer observations and share opinions. It might just keep us alive."

"Yes, Sir." Despite his best effort, Evans could tell he'd failed to disguise his bewilderment. He'd never before been sent on any special sort of assignment.

"The good news about reassignment is the increase in pay. The bad is, the odds of reaching retirement age have dramatically decreased. But, since you signed your life over to the government upon enlistment, Uncle Sam appreciates the sacrifice." Dutch grinned and slapped him on the back.

Evans flinched from the impact and issued another affirmative response.

Dutch tapped the video equipment inside the shoulder pack. "You've got the skills I need, son. Tonight's goal is simple. We're after confirmed reconnaissance of a specific subject. I want enough footage for the computer analysts to simulate specs on our guy's range of physical abilities."

Dutifully unzipping the pack, Evans slipped the equipment harness into place, strapped the camera in position and flipped on the record switch. "Does the target have specialized training, Sir?"

"You could say that, son. I've seen this bastard scale a sheer cliff as if he was a mountain goat, leap across a river

ALTERNATE ENDINGS

with the ease of a damn tiger and melt into the underbrush slicker than a coyote. He's a real legend." Dutch snorted out a grim laugh. "He moves like shadow in moonlight."

Evans pivoted in a slow arc, filming a test pattern across the black nightscape. He wished he had some clue as to what this was all about. He tried not to tense when he registered Dutch's suppressed amusement through the camera's viewfinder. He'd known something big was up soon after he'd reported as ordered. The strained expression on his Commanding Officer's face produced a sick dread, and the moment he'd been issued the immediate deployment orders, Evans had almost panicked. Being outfitted with requisitioned equipment was surreal, something that happened to other soldiers.

He adjusted the camera settings and studied Dutch. The black BDUs indicated some branch of elite Special Forces, but the man's collar was barren of insignia or rank. There was no mark of identity save for a subtle black-on-black embroidered shoulder patch, the design reminiscent of an ancient heraldic crest.

Dutch noticed his interest and curled his lips into a smirk. "Feeling clueless, Soldier?"

"Yes, Sir."

The man tapped the insignia on his shoulder. "St. George tasked a select few with a challenge." His voice resonated with a hint of menace.

Startled by the name, Evans blurted out the first association that came to mind. "He fought a dragon, Sir."

Dutch's nod was curt. "You know your history, Corporal. The misinformation is understandable considering public attitude regarding unicorns."

"Unicorns, Sir?" Evans stumbled over the word but his tone came out even and respectful.

"Yes, Corporal. The subject of tonight's objective is a unicorn." No mirth showed on Dutch's features now. "They're lethal. Forget that and you'll be dead before sunrise."

Evans gave good blank face, an ability which had always paid bonus dividends, but in his present situation he figured it saved him from a court martial.

Dutch rocked back on his heels and twisted a smile at him. "Questions, Corporal?"

"Yes, Sir. Uh, what makes the, ah, unicorn so dangerous?"

The black ops man nodded his approval. "Astute question, Corporal. Fairy tales have turned them into something soft and sweet but that's public relations bullshit. The truth is, they're vicious beasts."

Evans tried to freeze his facial muscles into a calm mask but it was a wasted effort and Dutch continued talking, warming to his theme.

"Evolution made them beautiful and lethal. Their hooves are natural weapons, sharp as chipped flint. The tail on an immature foal is whip-hard and the feathery wisps of hair can flay skin to the bone with a single swipe." He paused to scan the surrounding forest.

Nerves jangling, Evans caught himself doing the same. He couldn't restrain a little twitch when Dutch resumed his explanation.

"Mature males have venomous bites capable of causing instantaneous paralysis. During the gestation period, the females snort flames and the damned stuff acts just like napalm, sticky as jelly and burns hot as phosphorescence. They live for centuries and mate for life. Never get in the path of a subadult, they are deadly protective of offspring."

"Deadly." Evans echoed. Was his psych profile really whacked enough for this kind of detail?

Dutch waited until Evans' gaze steadied on his. "Remember that our adversaries exhibit superior speed and agility. Their intelligence is equal to our own. Never forget those deceptively lovely exteriors shield the moral ambiguity of a shark."

Evans sensed the ripple of movement and pivoted, drawing his firearm even as he continued to hold the camera in place. There was no sensory noise but he identified the shimmer of starlight reflecting off the sleek coat before his mind made sense of the visual.

It was another full second before Dutch reacted to his soft snort of disbelief.

The unicorn slid between the trunks of two massive trees. Steam issued in twin streams from his velvety nostrils. Smooth muscles glided as the stud danced forward, inky black cloven hooves taking delicate steps. Shining eyes, round as dark moons, scanned the men. His hide glowed with the iridescence of fine Burmese pearls. The single horn protruding from his forehead shone the deep blue of polished steel. The swirling ridges swept up to a tip sharp as a Falstaff. Fetlocks black as antique iron matched the creature's mane and exuded a masculine beauty storybooks had never captured.

"Halt." Evans' voice came out even, husky, and toneless.

The unicorn paused with his head tilted to one side, as if considering him with curiosity. After a lengthy perusal the beast pawed the earth, flung its mane, and rolled back its lips. The long beard trailing beneath the exposed strong white teeth and the sharp elongated canines of the stallion reflected in the dim light. The sight made Evan's mouth go dry and when a forked tongue slid out of the unicorn and tested the air like a snake might, he shuddered. He trained his firearm on the shining chest, but was caught unprepared by the beast's charge. He flung his body sideways and knocked Dutch into the roadside ditch, discharging his gun into the sky. Pain splintered his left bicep. He hit the ground and rolled into the wound, cradling his injured arm instinctively.

A silvery flash passed overhead.

The sharp horn had punctured his flesh.

Evans fingered the damage and then groped for the camera, climbing to his knees and filming as the animal cantered back into the forest.

Dutch crawled out the ditch and grinned at him.

Evans scowled back.

"Well done, Corporal. You're the first guy to survive the meet-and-greet." He climbed to his feet and jerked his head in the direction of where the unicorn had melted into the trees. "You've got good reflexes, son. Dodging strikes is tough." Dutch crossed the distance between them and grabbed a fistful of his uniform and hauled him up on his feet. "Time to go."

Fingers clutching the sleeve of Dutch's black BDU's, Evans staggered toward the vehicle. "That was a real unicorn, Sir." He slumped into the passenger side.

Dutch slapped a hand across Evans' forehead and pushed him against the seat back while he inspected the wound. He rummaged beneath the seat until he extracted a medical kit, knocking loose the latch and shaking out the supplies with one hand. He ripped the plastic wrap off a length of gauze with his teeth and wrapped the injury, cinching the ends tight.

"That was a unicorn, Sir. A real unicorn." Evans repeated.

"Yes it was, Corporal." Dutch unstrapped the camera from the shoulder straps and tossed it on top of the bag behind the passenger seat. "You're lucky he caught you in the torso. I couldn't do much for the last guy that got pulled for this type of detail. Poor bastard got skewered through the groin."

Evans grimaced. His wound didn't seem so bad in light of that news.

Dutch climbed behind the steering wheel and started the engine. "Just you wait, son. Unicorns are nothing compared to a pissed off pixie."

ABOUT THE AUTHOR

As an anthropologist, Lesann Berry divides her time between academic interests and professional research. Focused primarily on the American west, she is inspired by the geologic features of empty landscapes. The ancient art and prehistory of those settings often feature in her work. She writes about messed-up people and sinister events, saying her stories often feature paranormal or romantic elements because life is boring without spooky stuff and warm bodies. Crossing genre lines, she pens both contemporary and historical mysteries, romantic suspense, and even a little horror.

Visit WWW.LESANNBERRY.COM for new releases.

Made in the USA
Lexington, KY
09 December 2015